THE
Autumn Wife

LISA
ANN VERGE

Publishing History

Print edition published by Bay Street Press
Copyright © 2025 Lisa Ann Verge
ISBN: 978-1-940963-33-4
Editing: Joyce Lamb
Cover design by The Killion Group

About The Autumn Wife and the King's Girls Series

The stories in the King's Girls Series are inspired by real events. For those interested, here's the history behind the novels.

In 1663, the tiny, just-burgeoning colony of Quebec was dominated by rowdy young men in search of exploration and adventure, much to the chagrin of their French King, who had big ambitions.

To settle his far-roaming countrymen, King Louis XIV chose young women from orphanages and the French countryside, girls he honored by calling them his daughters. He gifted them dowries appropriate to frontier life and then shipped them off to present-day Canada to be married.

Eight hundred women sailed to the unbroken wilderness between 1663 and 1673. Known as *Filles du Roi*, they are now the honored maternal ancestors of a large portion of modern-day, French-speaking Quebecois.

Their stories are true—mine are fiction, inspired by their courage, boldness, and spirit.

Also by Lisa Ann Verge

King's Girls Series
HEAVEN IN HIS ARMS
THE WINTER HUSBAND
THE AUTUMN WIFE
A HUSBAND BY CHRISTMAS

The Celtic Legends Series
TWICE UPON A TIME: Book One
THE FAERY BRIDE: Book Two
WILD HIGHLAND MAGIC: Book Three
THE CELTIC LEGENDS SERIES: BOX SET
THE O'MADDEN: A Novella

Stand Alone Historical Romance
HER PIRATE HEART
SING ME HOME
THE CAPTIVE KNIGHT
ROMANTIC JOURNEYS COLLECTION: BOX SET

Writing as Lisa Verge Higgins

THE PROPER CARE AND MAINTENANCE OF
FRIENDSHIP
ONE GOOD FRIEND DESERVES ANOTHER
FRIENDSHIP MAKES THE HEART GROW
FONDER
RANDOM ACTS OF KINDNESS
SENSELESS ACTS OF BEAUTY

CHAPTER ONE

Convent of Notre Dame
Montreal, July 29, 1673

Far across the grassy lawn, Cecile glimpsed her precious boy about to be crushed into a bloody pulp.

With a choking scream, she took off, skirts flying, bolting toward the construction site of a half-built chapel. She shouted a warning, but Etienne, ignorant of his approaching death, kept chattering with a cluster of young laborers nearby. Glaring at the stone block about to fall upon his head, panic in her throat, she tried to will the rock to slow down. Shiny bits in the surface winked at her, mocking her as it rotated in its tumble.

Look up! Etienne!

Etienne's head shot up—she glimpsed the angry scratch across his chin from the fall he'd taken that very morning, when he'd pulled the canoe up to the riverbank of these convent grounds. She glimpsed the dark mole above his lip, and watched his eyes narrow in question as the shadow of the rock darkened his shoulder.

A word ripped up her throat. *Mooooooooooove!*

Then a blur swept past her field of vision. In one moment, Etienne's face blazed in her sight, and in the next, the stone tumbling from the highest point of the unfinished façade slammed into the ground. Clods, shards, and dust billowed. With a sharp cry, she stopped as if she'd been struck herself. Teetering with her arms flung out, she gaped at the curtain of dirt that obscured the building site. From that cloud came a man's shout, a boy's squeal, but no voice that resonated in her bones like the pitch of Etienne's cry.

Etienne.

How many times over the past years had she rushed to save him? How many times had she been too late to throw herself between his father's whistling leather belt and the boy's narrow back? Had she failed again? How could Etienne die like this, after all they'd been through, this boy, the light of her life?

The veil of dust dimmed and then she saw it— the flash of a knobby knee emerging from the torn, buff-colored breeches of a bending leg. Gasping, she hurled herself toward him, shouting his name.

Sprawled on the stone-strewn ground of the building site, Theo turned at the sound of a shriek. He glimpsed, coming through the haze, a froth of kicked-up skirts, white ruffles, a blur of yellow like the colza flowers that bloomed on the mountainsides of his hometown of Guéret. Those skirts drifted down as a young woman threw herself onto her knees beside the boy he'd just shoved out of mortal danger. On the breeze of her pace flowed a wildflower scent, cutting through the ashen stink of the lime ricks.

"Are you hurt?" The woman's hands fluttered over the boy's cheeks, shoulders, and arms like little white birds. She gasped at the sight of his bleeding forearm.

"Don't fuss." The boy eased himself up to a sitting position and cast a lowered glance toward the gaping apprentices. "It's just a scrape."

"You're lucky to be alive." The woman's voice quivered like a taut-drawn violin string. "Did I not tell you to wait on the bench outside the convent while I met with Mother Superior?" She hauled in a frustrated breath. "The meeting hadn't even begun. I was inside the building only a minute before I poked my head out to see you—to *not* see you—"

"It wasn't his fault." Theo took pity on the young man, mortified under the barrage of the public scolding. "I was on the road; I saw it all happen. The mason on the ladder wasn't wearing a leather bib—"

"Hey!"

Theo glanced toward the sound of the voice and saw the fool he'd just been talking about. The redheaded mason leaped down from the last rung of the rickety ladder and strode toward him, gesturing toward the boy. "He was standing where he wasn't supposed to be."

"He is alive, sir, only because of the efforts of this man." The woman flung the words like javelins. "Alive," she repeated, "with no thanks to you."

Pushing himself up to his knees, Theo took a keener look at the beauty talking like a general. Seeing such a genteel lady in this frontier settlement was a rare thing, but this woman was of the kind who would seize the attention of any man anywhere in the world. A tiny nose, a rosy mouth, delicate features at war with her fierce expression. She wasn't wearing the common gray habit of the novices, but rather, a well-tailored dress and fine linen scarf embroidered with green climbing vines. She might have leaped into his vision straight from a maypole ceremony outside his parish church.

There it was again, his past, sneaking up on him.

A life stolen.

Theo drove the thought away as he rose to his feet and held out a hand to help the lady up. She didn't glance at his outstretched arm, or even turn her head to acknowledge his presence. Instead, she tugged her skirts from under her knees, canted back on her heels, and rose on her own power to a height not much taller than his shoulder.

She took a step closer to the redheaded mason, shards of rock crunching beneath her boots. "Have you nothing to say for yourself, sir?"

"Like I told you…." Nostrils flaring, the mason jutted his chin toward the still-sprawled boy. "He shouldn't have been hanging around here. Neither should strangers coming off the road."

Theo braced himself for a fight, but the woman spoke first.

"Those apprentices"—the woman gestured toward the younger laborers still mixing mortar in a trough—"work just as close to the wall as my boy was standing. Any laborer on this site could have been walking by that ladder."

"Anyone with *sense*," the mason corrected, "would have kept a proper distance."

Theo stepped between them, diverting the man's attention to someone his own size. Fighting would get Theo in a heap of trouble, but such insolence to the fairer sex begged a response. "That wall," Theo began, thrusting his hand out toward the half-built façade of the chapel, "is, what, twenty feet high? So, where's the scaffolding? The bucket-pulley? And where's your overseer?"

The mason scowled and looked him over. Theo stiffened, keenly aware that his tattered woolen vest and ragged breeches marked him as the lowest of men. In France, he'd been a respected craftsman. Here, the law called him an indentured servant but the brute who held his papers treated him like a slave.

"You," the mason spat. "You're telling me my job?"

"If I were your overseer, I'd demote you to mixing mortar with those apprentices."

"Ha!" The mason looked him up and down. "Some master's dog giving me orders?"

Theo's hands curled into fists. The taunting and the disrespect—spoken in front of a lady like this—fueled a powerful urge to strike the smirk from the mason's face. Just the thought of swinging a fist shot such a thrill through him that he took a step forward—

He stopped short as the lady herself slid half in front of him in a scent-cloud of violets.

"There has been enough blood spilled today, sirs." Her voice had lost some of its fury but was buttressed by steel. "No fisticuffs. I insist."

Inwardly, he grunted, loath to back down. The mason taunted him, doubling down with a slow, daring smile. But Theo pulled back on his fury. The lady's intervention had saved him. If he involved himself in any kind of violence—no matter how justified—he'd be slapped back in shackles, tied to a pole for a whipping—or, worse, have another year added to his term of indentured servitude.

Twelve weeks and one day.

Then he'd be free.

A cool, smooth hand lightly brushed his forearm. A moment later, he found himself staring at those pale fingers as they retreated from his grit-strewn wrist. As he shifted his attention to her face, he stilled. Her amber-bright gaze slammed into him like an anchor into the sea bottom.

"That cut on your head needs tending, sir." She stepped back with a tilt of her head. "Come with me, please."

CHAPTER TWO

Cecile looked up at the man who'd just saved Etienne's life.

Smeared with stone-dust and pebbled with shards, the towering laborer brought to mind the sheer, carved rock face of Quebec City. The forearm she'd barely brushed had felt solid with knotted muscle. His palms bore calluses. His tattered breeches molded to swelling thighs. Deep-set eyes beamed, embers of fury still burning bright inside them, and now that intensity bathed her in an unsettling way.

Had she bumped into this man on the streets of the nearby settlement of Montreal, she'd have choked down a scream and raced as far away from him as possible. But no matter how dangerous he appeared, he had just saved a life more important than her own. The least she could do was tend his wounds.

"Come," she repeated, shrinking away from the size and heat of him. "They'll have linens and ointments at the convent."

She swiveled around on a heel, slung an arm over Etienne's shoulders, and propelled her boy along a grass-flattened path toward the main convent building. The disconcerting man followed with a frustrated, dragging tread. The mason was the one who'd nearly started a fight, but the man behind her had seemed keen enough to join in the violence.

Dear heavens, did *every* man in this rough settlement walk about with a belly of dry tinder, so easily lit? At least Etienne was safe now. Pulling the boy closer to her side, she scolded herself to be grateful to Etienne's savior, no matter how frightful and intimidating he looked.

To calm herself, she took another hard look at the convent grounds. She hoped this collection of rough buildings would become the sanctuary that she and Etienne so desperately needed. It seemed isolated enough, though the settlement of Montreal proper was only a short walk west. The wide, grassy clearing was hemmed by forest on either side. The lawn unfurled from the banks of the Saint Lawrence River all the way up to the dirt road that ran parallel to the river at the top of a gentle slope.

The construction site for the chapel lay beside that road. A small distance behind stood the main convent building they were approaching, sturdily built of logs, but no majestic thing. She'd been told it served as both living quarters for the nuns and a school for local girls. She could only surmise that two additional outbuildings on the opposite side of the field were used for storage or perhaps lodging for the laborers. Cecile couldn't help comparing this congregation to the Salpêtrière Orphanage in Paris, with its domed chapel, stone courtyard, and four floors of cloistered lodgings, where she'd been raised.

Rough and small, this convent, but certainly the kindly Reverend Mother could arrange for a seat in a monastery school for Etienne, and, for a widow like herself, protection from the world.

As well as the law.

She approached a bench set against the convent wall and gestured to it. "Here we are. Have a seat, both of you."

Etienne shrugged out of her grip and threw himself onto the bench. The laborer sat with more dignity. Cecile hadn't so forgotten her upbringing that she would ignore the proprieties, so she summoned the courage to look the rugged stranger in the face— but not any higher than his bristled chin.

"Sir." Breath gathered in her chest. "I have been negligent in thanking you for saving this disobedient boy from terrible harm."

"He would have stepped away in time." The man shrugged, his rumbling voice rising from that tremendous chest as if from an abyss. "Boys move quickly at that age."

"When they're paying attention, perhaps." She glanced at a slouching Etienne, partly to remove the muscle-bound man from her sight, and partly to pin the boy with her displeasure. "This young man was too intent on assaulting people with questions to realize a boulder was soon to fall on his head. Do you have nothing to say to the man who saved your life, Etienne?"

Etienne frowned. A hank of dark hair fell over his brow to shield his eyes—yes, he knew he was wrong—but then, just as quickly, he straightened on his seat with a swagger. "Sir." Etienne bowed toward his bench mate, adding with a voice full of drama, "I owe you my life."

She opened her mouth to scold him for flippancy—a new quality since he'd recently turned fourteen, and not a good one—but before she could, the man grunted, "Nonsense."

Nonsense? Saving a life was certainly *not* nonsense—she would have thrown herself under that stone. She gave the stranger a side look to see if his expression matched his humble tone, but now he was squinting toward the wooded horizon.

"The boy is safe," he said with another shrug of those intimidating shoulders. "No need for thanks."

"You've earned my gratitude whether you think it's necessary or not." She glared at Etienne, who was now *grinning*, oblivious to the fact that she'd nearly died herself, watching his bloody demise unfold before her eyes. "Allow me to introduce myself. I am Madame Tremblay."

The man's head swiveled toward her—clearly surprised at the word *Madame*, she suspected, because it marked her as married. Not that this man had shown even a glimmer of crude interest. So far, he'd been gentlemanly, polite. But in a settlement where there were hundreds of frontiersmen for every one Frenchwoman, she opted to be forever wary.

"Theo," the stranger said with a slight bow of his head. "Theo Martin."

"Monsieur Martin, it's our great fortune to have met you." Since the proprieties had been seen to, she switched to a safer, motherly tone of voice. "The sisters live in this building, so no men are allowed inside, but I must fetch linens and water. I'll return in a moment to tend to your wounds. Don't you dare move, Etienne, not an inch."

Passing by the seated Theo Martin, she breathed in the scent of stone dust and pine sap rising from him before darting through the door into the safety of the convent. Inside the dim vestibule—alone at last— she collapsed against the door and slid down to a crouch.

Squeezing her arms around her midriff, gripped by nausea, she succumbed to all the banked feelings. Reliving the sight of Etienne almost dying made sweat burst upon her brow and her body tremble. She flung her arms around her knees and drew them in so she wouldn't shatter into a thousand pieces. Up came all the old fears, too, the nightmare terrors, the seared-in memory of belt-snaps that made her flinch even now.

Sister Anne suddenly swept into the vestibule. "Ah, Madame Tremblay, you're back. By the saints! Are you sick?"

"No, no." Cecile released her grip on her knees, forced her back straight, and shoved herself upright on numb, shaking legs. "I…I just stepped outside for a moment. I…I witnessed an accident at the building site."

"Another?" The sister clattered the rosary beads in her hand. "That would be six times this week. What happened?"

"A stone fell from on high." She shouldn't mention Etienne—lest he be blamed—and also because that might affect her plans. "A man swept in to save the…the boy beneath."

"Heaven's gates. Thank God for that brave man. How bad are the injuries?"

"Just scratches, I think." Breathing deeply, she willed herself to focus on what needed to be done. "Would you have some clean linens, Sister Anne? Fresh water? Perhaps some ointment?"

"Yes, yes, we've stocked up on such things since the building began." With a flurry, the sister slipped back into the main schoolroom, saying over her shoulder, "Much obliged, Madame Tremblay, for seeing to the wounded. I dare not send one of our young novices to those wolves."

By the time the nun returned with a bowl, salve, and linens, Cecile had deep-breathed herself to a hard-earned, somewhat steady calm. She stepped outside to the sight of Etienne shooting question after question at Theo Martin.

"I apologize, sir." She passed by the laborer and sank onto the bench on the far side of Etienne. "Etienne has many good qualities, but he can be impertinent in his curiosity."

Etienne's jaw took on a defiant cast. "Mr. Martin was telling me about the different kinds of stone. He's a mason."

Inwardly, she started. That had to be a lie. Masonry was a rare skill in these settlements—anyone who had even an hour of experience would find himself much in demand. If this Theo Martin was a mason, he'd be working as one in Montreal or Quebec and wearing better clothes. Like breeches that weren't strained to bursting around those massive thighs.

"I *used* to be a mason," the man corrected in a low, reluctant tone. "But that was a long time ago."

None of this was her business, so she wet a linen and said, "Lift your arm, Etienne."

"But once you're a mason," Etienne ventured, exposing the scratches that she set to swabbing, "aren't you a stonemason for life?"

The man paused. Cecile didn't have to look his way to sense his discomfort.

Etienne, oblivious of the thickening atmosphere, forged ahead, turning to speak to her. "Monsieur Martin was apprenticed at my age. Maybe *I* can be apprenticed as a mason, too? Then I could work here, at the chapel building site. What do you think?"

She ducked her head, seeking bloody rips in the back of Etienne's dust-smeared shirt as her heart squeezed. Since she and Etienne had been evicted from their home in Trois-Rivières, Etienne had come up with a dozen ways he could hire himself out. He stated that he was old enough to work and could support them both with his wages. She hated the truth in his words, as well as the idea of Etienne doing hard labor. Despite the thin mustache growing over that mole above his mouth, he would always be a boy in her eyes. A brilliant boy who deserved the education that had formerly—unfairly—been denied to him.

"Don't fuss with the bindings." She ignored Etienne's question as she finished wrapping his forearm. "I'll check it later."

Etienne sat up straight. "When we get back to Captain Girard's house?"

She frowned at his hopeful gleefulness. Etienne didn't like her plan to come here and ask favors of Mother Superior. He had begged to stay at the Girards' *seigneurie* with its endless woods and the captain he worshipped. But that place had been a temporary refuge—they wouldn't be safe there indefinitely.

Sighing, she stood up and set the bowl of water against her hip. "I still have to talk to Mother Superior, Etienne. You know this is for the best."

Stepping around him, she approached the so-called mason, sprawled with his eyes closed against the wall of the schoolhouse. Swallowing down nerves, she told herself this stranger couldn't hurt her, not out in the open like this. But, truly, when would her bones stop rattling at the very hint of a threat? This man was a fearsome sight, with blood caked on his temple and jaw, dampened by beads of sweat. The folds of his shirt molded against his rippling abdomen, and his strong legs went on forever.

Despite his assertion of being a mason, he was likely a simple laborer. Though not many laborers had board-straight shoulders like this. Most were bowed and broken by tough work, like felling trees or hauling stumps out of the ground. And his teeth were strong, white, and well cared for—which she noticed as he suddenly smiled.

"The blood there," she blurted, gesturing to his shirt as if it were the blood she'd been staring at. "Is it all from your head wound? I don't see any wounds anywhere else."

"Don't know."

His eyes slitted against the sun. He pushed himself up straighter within her shadow, probing the wound on his temple with dirty fingers.

"Stop." She slapped his hand away. Her palm stung. So did her audacity. "You'll—you'll only make it worse."

In her shadow, his eyes lost their squint. Green eyes, she noticed. Or gray. A color like the edge of thick glass.

Get hold of yourself. Water sloshed out of the bowl at her hip as she startled. *Don't be a coward.*

"Keep your head down, sir." She planted the bowl of water on the bench and pushed his thick, dark hair off his brow less gently than she ought to. The smell of crushed pine needles and something metallic rose up from his body. "Stay still while I clean this."

Despite her orders, he leaned back a fraction to catch Etienne's eye. "Bossy, isn't she?"

Etienne barked a laugh. "You don't know the half of it."

"Not bossy enough." Her voice went shrewish, and she didn't care. "Perhaps, if I were firmer in my discipline, I wouldn't be here tending to both of your wounds."

Etienne made a sound in the back of his throat. "I *said* I was *sorry.* I shouldn't have gone over there."

"I hope, the next time," she said, dipping a linen in the water, "you will consider how sorry *I* would be if something were to happen to you, Etienne."

The man flinched under her touch. She pulled her hand away from where she was swiping, but he didn't appear to be in pain—just annoyed.

"Etienne," he said, in a low voice. "Listen to her. She's right. It's clear your sister loves you."

"Sister?" Etienne hooted. "I have no sister. She's my mother."

CHAPTER THREE

The boy's *mother?*

Impossible. The two of them couldn't be ten years apart in age. Yet Theo had witnessed how the woman had drawn the boy tight against her side earlier and how the boy—despite his struggle to act unaffected—had, for a brief moment, let his head fall against her shoulder. Theo had assumed they were children of a different father or mother. The boy was lanky, dark-haired, black-eyed, his complexion more Huron than French.

The woman was all sunshine. Her fair blonde hair was gathered at the nape of a neck that looked too slender to hold the weight of motherhood. Her pale skin looked as soft as clouds.

Only her eyes were dark. Swirling shades of earthy brown, like the chocolate in a porcelain cup that had been served to him once, back when he'd been allowed to visit the house of the man who'd fathered him.

"I *am* Etienne's mother, sir, in all but blood." The lady spoke the words like he'd pulled them out of her, then returned to poking at his wound with a wet linen. "Etienne is the son of my husband and his late wife."

Ah, a stepmother. That explained the narrow age gap. The strength of the affection between the two ran deep—not always the case, as he knew very well from his own home situation.

"My mistake," he said, tilting his head to give her better access to his wound. "But mother or sister, what I said still runs true. Etienne, a good son gives his worried mother no trouble."

Like he hadn't caused his own mother a heap of trouble before he'd been exiled across an ocean.

"You will have a scar, Monsieur Martin." Her voice tightened as she shifted the topic of conversation. "A small one, but it'll leave a ridge."

Like yours? His gaze slid to a scar and small divot by her hairline.

"Perhaps," she continued, "if I bind the wound—"

"Don't bother." Returning to his master's land with his head bound by a bloody linen would invite a thousand questions. "Stop the bleeding as best as you can and I'll get back on the road. I've got business in Montreal."

He nudged her hand away and felt her retreat more than was warranted by a brief touch. Curious, he dared to meet those wary brown eyes. Damn, she was a beauty. In another time, a better place—when he had something to offer a woman other than a night's pleasure—he would have flirted with her. The urge rose up in him, but he pushed it back down. Not only was she cringing at their proximity—and trying not to—she was also married.

That his mind strayed in that direction was proof that he'd been too long without a woman. Best to avoid entanglements of any kind, when in twelve weeks and a day he would settle old scores and atone for the trouble he'd left behind.

Suddenly, the door to the schoolhouse creaked open on leather hinges. He glanced over to see two nuns stride out into the blaze of the July day.

Unfolding to his full height, he bowed to the holy women. Madame Tremblay splashed the bloody linen into the bowl before she stepped up beside him—an arm's length away and then some. How ill at ease she was with him.

"Madame Tremblay," the leading nun said, "it's kind of you to step in and help the injured. Not all visitors are so eager to play the good Samaritan."

"Of course," the lady replied in a warmer voice than she had used with him. "Mother Superior, I assume?"

The nun nodded and gestured toward him. "Is this our hero?"

The nun gave Theo a thorough perusal. He braced himself for the look that always came after—the scornful dismissal of a man of no consequence—but when the nun's gaze returned to his face, he saw only curiosity and gratitude in those blue eyes.

"Forgive my rudeness," Mother Superior said, "but I do not recognize you. I had expected—well, *hoped*—that the responsible party to today's heroics might be one of the workers on my project."

Her project?

In his experience, it was always the local bishop or a head monk who financed and planned religious building projects, even for convents. Frontier life required such a shattering of norms, he supposed—and the Reverend Mother had clearly risen to the challenge. Though he'd noticed a few flaws in mortaring—the fault of the workers—and a lack of safety—the fault of the building overseer—the building site itself was highly organized. Bluestone had been set aside in neat rows for sills and lintels. The best Pointe-aux-Trembles limestone was being crushed to make mortar. Taking everything in, he had lingered on the roadside, gawping with envy at the working masons, losing himself in memories of better days when he'd been tasked to raise castles and cathedrals under his bare hands.

"Monsieur?" the Reverend Mother prodded. "Your name?"

"Theo Martin," he stated, bending his neck. "I happened to be passing by when I witnessed the accident—the near accident."

"Well, I'm very glad the Holy Spirit nudged you in the right direction. There have been too many injuries on this project. The prayers of my congregation are powerful, but"—she shook her white-capped head—"those workers could help the angels a little, by paying more attention to safety."

"Reverend Mother." The boy Etienne shoved off the wooden bench and took a swaggering step to his mother's side. "The mason who dropped the stone wasn't wearing a leather bib. And the stone was too heavy to carry without it."

"Is that so?" A smile twitched at the corners of the nun's lips. "And who is this well-informed young gentleman?"

Theo didn't have to turn his head to sense Madame Tremblay stiffening like a lioness beside her cub.

He did wonder why, though.

The lady said, "This is Etienne Tremblay, the boy who was saved. He's my"—her voice caught on a breath—"he's my son."

"Oh?" The nun blinked. "My dear lady, unless the angel Gabriel appeared to you as a child, this young man must be adopted."

"A stepson," Theo offered. The hot sun glanced off the golden surface of her hair, nearly blinding him.

But not so much that he didn't notice the tendons standing out in the lady's throat.

What worried her so much?

"I saw everything," Etienne blurted, rising to his toes. "I was supposed to wait here, on the bench. But I..." The boy cast a glance toward the bustling worksite. "I was curious about the construction."

"That's where I saw him," Theo added as Madame Tremblay bit her lower lip hard. A lady in distress had always been his weakness. "I witnessed one of the masons carrying a stone that was too large to be hauled up a ladder that was too rickety to use, especially for such weight."

The Reverend Mother bent her head back. "And what do you know of such things?"

Everything.

"I grew up in a village of stonemasons, and was apprenticed from a young age." He flexed his empty hands, aching to hold a trowel. "I spent years in Paris building cathedrals."

"Wait..." The nun leaned in, setting the cross at her neck swinging. "You're a *mason?*"

"Yes, or at least I was, back in France." His shoulders straightened with a pride he couldn't afford to have or show off. "I'm a master mason."

The boastful words launched out of him, propelled not only by the realization that this nun was in charge of the chapel-building project, but also by the awareness of the lovely woman standing by his side. The woman who'd tended him out of decency and politeness, but who'd done so with visible wariness. Probably because she saw him as only a dirty laborer. How fine it would be for such a woman to see him as the better man, the craftsman he had been, back when he was deserving of respect.

Respect was the very first thing he'd lost.

"A master mason?" The nun clutched the wooden cross to stop its swinging. "Saints alive, I have scoured the settlement looking for masons. My own overseer just quit, lured away by the bishop in the upper city of Quebec, who promised him a grander project. Who do you work for?"

"I don't work as a mason." He tightened his jaw, trying to find a way to tell this nun the truth without lowering himself in the lady's eyes. "The man who holds my papers"—*of indentured servitude*—"prefers I clear timber and stumps from his land. He has no interest in stone buildings."

"What a terrible waste of talent." The Reverend Mother gestured toward the building site. "What's your opinion of our chapel, then? Be honest."

Considering the gulf between his appearance and his claims, he shouldn't take umbrage that the nun would test his knowledge about construction. But it always struck him like a mallet how little trust he now commanded. "The footprint is solid," he began, "and your overseer has kept it well organized. But there are stones in the south-facing wall that are set on the wrong side of the grain. And two of the furnaces over there—the lime ricks—have sputtered out. They should be burning limestone continually so there's a steady supply for the mortar."

In the wake of his words, he sensed a shift in the lovely Madame Tremblay's attention. He stood a little straighter.

"Goodness, a prayer is sent up and then answered in the most unexpected way." With a swift hand, Mother Superior made the sign of the cross. "Sir, tell me who holds your papers."

"Monsieur Rivard." He couldn't say that name without swallowing a surge of bile. "He has a landholding a half day's canoe ride downstream."

"Would he hire you out, do you think?"

"I…" *Doubt it.* "I don't know."

"Well, then, I ask you: Would you like to work on the building site for my chapel? I'm in need of an overseer."

An overseer.

The world went fuzzy, shivered, and doubled. He could almost feel the smooth handle of a trowel sliding into his palm, the jolt of a shovel against limestone, the creak of wooden scaffolding under his feet. His chest swelled, filling with that most dangerous sensation—a bubbling stew of hope, anticipation, and expectation.

He struggled to press it down, deflate it. He was not his own man, and his master would sooner whip him than give up the labor of his strong back. But one flit of a glance at the woman by his side—one catch of her bright-amber gaze uplifted—and all struggles ceased.

So much had been stolen from him. Freedom, friends, family.

This nun offered a chance to seize back some respect.

"Yes," he blurted. "I'd be happy to work for you."

CHAPTER FOUR

Cecile stood motionless as Mother Superior related details of the chapel project to the soon-to-be-hired, dangerously strong laborer. No, not a common laborer, but a *master mason* just as he'd told Etienne. The proof became apparent the more he spoke. Gesturing here and there, he talked about stones, and wall construction, and building safety. He held the Reverend Mother's fascinated attention and tugged at Cecile's own. But Monsieur Martin's metamorphosis from a strongman laborer into a master craftsman, though astounding, wasn't any of her concern. Etienne's accident had interrupted her plans, but she'd come to this convent for a purpose too important to delay any longer.

At a pause in the conversation, Cecile leaned in. "Reverend Mother—"

"A moment, my dear." The nun held up a finger. "Sir, by the time you finish your errands in Montreal, I'll have written the letter to Monsieur Rivard for you to pick up. Deliver the letter to your master yourself and urge him to let you come to our building site as soon as possible."

The mason dipped his head in assent.

"Now, Madame Tremblay." The nun turned to Cecile. "We have an appointment, do we not?"

Cecile nodded.

"Unfortunately, I have little time. I returned here from France only a week ago, my desk is overflowing with unreconciled accounts and unanswered correspondence, and soon I'll be off to Quebec once again, likely to fight with the bishop. I believe we should put off our conversation for a few weeks until—"

"Please, Mother." Cecile's ribs squeezed. "I've come all the way from Trois-Rivières to see you. I promise I shall be brief."

The nun's ample chest rose and fell but her eyes softened. "I suppose, like my namesake Saint Martha, I shouldn't be so consumed by worldly worries." She glanced at her ink-stained fingers then, with a shrug, swiveled in a twist of gray serge. "Come, madame, let's talk in the garden."

Cecile's pulse leapt with renewed hope. "Wait here, Etienne." She ignored her son's huff as he hurled himself onto the bench. Cecile passed the soon-to-be overseer, summoning enough courage to say as a parting gesture, "Your wound has stopped bleeding, sir. Do try to keep it clean."

Cecile trotted away faster than she probably should, turning at the corner of the building in time to catch up with the nun. Behind the convent schoolhouse, the Reverend Mother stopped just outside a rough fence that encircled a garden, the stalks of corn visible over the edge.

"Here." Mother Superior took two reed-woven baskets from a pile and held one out to Cecile. "I planned to do this later in the afternoon when the heat has waned, but we can talk as we gather."

Cecile slid the handle over her arm as she followed the nun through the gate, the fecund aroma of soil filling her head. They walked through the clusters of maize, twined with bean tendrils, the ground beneath covered with sprawling squash. The Three Sisters, as the local tribes dubbed them, were being grown in the native way. Nostalgia for her own garden seeped through her. Unlike this well-tended space, her garden had likely long gone weed-choked and wild in the hands of her husband's creditors.

Mother Superior paused in dappled light on the middle path. "Some of the beans are ripe, and I'm told the blackberry bushes should be pushing early fruit." The nun turned a merry eye toward her. "I confess I'm craving Sister Anne's blackberry crisp. It's been two years since I've tasted her version. That's how long I've been away from here, trying to get royal and ecclesiastical approval for our little congregation."

"Sister Anne told me how grateful she is that you have returned." Cecile debated whether to tell the Reverend Mother that it was the news of the nun's arrival that had birthed Cecile's unlikely plan. She quickly decided against it. The better tactic would be to put Mother Superior in a generous mood before asking for two tremendous favors. "Your arrival brought great luck, Mother, since you've found a master mason to be your overseer."

"Yes, and only days after the former overseer departed. Proof of a prayer answered." The corn being too green, the nun turned her attention to the bean pods dangling from vines. "That chapel has been nearly twenty years in the making, you know. Only by the grace of God has it gotten this far. In France, I was compelled to make a promise to my superiors that it will be completed in time to be consecrated in the spring, so there's much work to be done." As the sister snapped off a bean pod at the stem, Cecile wasn't sure whether the nun was talking to her or herself. "Yet how is it to be finished, I wonder, if I keep losing skilled laborers to much larger projects in Quebec? Which is a long way of saying, Madame Tremblay, that, before meeting your Monsieur Martin—"

My Monsieur Martin?

"—I was in terrible, desperate straits." Mother Superior snapped off another bulging pod and tossed it in Cecile's basket. "As, I suspect you are, too."

The nun's look pierced right through her. The nun *couldn't* know the extent of Cecile's desperation. The Reverend Mother was the holiest of holy women, but surely the sister couldn't discern, just with a look, all the sins that had driven Cecile to this convent today.

"My dear lady, you've gone ashen." The nun plunged a hand into a pocket of her skirts. "When was the last time you ate?"

Cecile had eaten sagamité with dried blueberries at the Girards' this morning, before she and Etienne had climbed into the canoe, but she couldn't remember tasting a thing. "It's just the heat, I think."

"This July has been stifling. God help the laborers outside." The nun tilted her head in the general direction of muffled clanging and shouts. "They've been working all day under that burning sky. Here, this might help." The nun lifted her hand. Something small and amber gleamed in her palm. "These sweets are the best medicine, no matter what the ailment."

Cecile took the offering, a boiled maple syrup candy.

"I keep a bag of them in my office, my little indulgence." The nun wrinkled her nose over a puckish grin. "The flood of papers always on that desk stirs up dust, and that makes me cough."

Cecile weighed the candy gleaming between her fingertips and found herself thrust back to a chilly October day in the open market of Montreal just after she was married. She had raced to the blanket of a Huron trader, drawn by the irresistible scent of maple…only to be yanked away by her cursing husband, who smelled like he'd spent her dowry on sour wine.

"Taste it." The nun jerked her chin to the candy. "It'll do you good. Maybe even loosen whatever confession you've got bottled up inside you."

Color rising, Cecile slipped the sweet between her lips. As the smooth flavor blossomed, a prickling began behind her eyes. She'd spent so many years in isolation. Kindness from strangers was an unfamiliar thing. And how would Cecile thank this kind nun for her compassion? With a mangled story of half-truths and lies.

To think she had once been an honest woman.

"My husband abandoned me and Etienne." She spoke around the lump of candy, then tucked it between cheek and tooth to melt on its own. "The last time I saw Eduard was more than eighteen months ago, when he set off into the wilderness on a trading trip."

"I see." The nun slid her piercing gaze away, turning back to the bean vine to inspect more pods for ripeness. "Your husband is a woods runner, then."

Acid splashed up to her mouth. She sucked harder on the candy to douse the burn. Woods runners were known to be ungovernable and freedom-loving. Yet Cecile had been sent to these settlements by the King of France himself—along with hundreds of other King's Girls—to marry the very kind of men who didn't want to marry in the first place.

Keep with the story.

"Usually," Cecile continued as a drop of sweat slid down her temple, "my husband would return home in late spring or early summer. But he has not made an appearance."

A river of lines deepened on the nun's brow. "Surely you know that woods runners will stay abroad if they haven't gathered enough furs to make the venture profitable. His long absence is hardly proof of abandonment—"

"I have reason to believe otherwise."

"Oh?"

She forced the well-practiced words to her lips. "My husband had many creditors. Several were owed such large amounts that they pooled their resources and sent a search party to find him. The search party traveled two months west, as far as Chequamegon Bay, on the far end of a lake so enormous it's like an inland sea."

"It's a vast wilderness, my dear." The nun shrugged. "He could still be hiding."

"He's not hiding."

The cords of her throat drew taut. She sucked deeply on the maple candy, shuddering at her own audacity. She slid her gaze down from the wary perusal of the nun, only for it to fall upon the wooden cross around the sister's neck.

I am going to hell.

"When the search party returned," she continued, pushing through her well-rehearsed story, "the creditors descended upon my home in Trois-Rivières." A tremor rattled through her as she remembered how two of Eduard's furious partners had burst through the door of her one-room cabin, bristling with weapons, smelling like bears. "They told me they were within the law to seize everything my husband owned in order to pay his long-overdue debts…including what he owed gambling. They confiscated our chickens and our house and our land."

The nun tossed more beans in Cecile's basket as she let loose a grunt of disapproval.

"The men in the search party," Cecile continued, "told my husband's creditors that there were multiple witnesses who swore my husband had died in the wilderness." She made an effort to look pained, but she'd never been a good pretender, even in her orphanage's annual nativity play. "So here I am, without a husband, three months without a home, without income…and with a son to support."

"Oh, what trouble men cause in their sinfulness." The Reverend Mother clucked her tongue. "My condolences for your loss, my dear, whether he abandoned you or has met his Maker. Where have you been staying since you were evicted?"

"Etienne and I found refuge with my former schoolmate, Marie"—darling Marie, Cecile would be friendless without her—"and her husband, Captain Lucas Girard, in their *seigneurie* upstream from here."

"Ah, yes, I am acquainted with them. Lovely family. Generous contributors to our congregation, as well as the building fund for that chapel."

"The Girards have been gracious hosts," Cecile added, "but I cannot impose upon their generosity forever. I have no family here, Etienne's father has no family here, and, alas, we know nothing about Etienne's Huron mother's family. So, I've come here today"—she scraped up all the hope and courage she could muster—"to ask if you could secure my son a placement in a monastery residential school in Montreal."

The Reverend Mother tossed more pods into the basket, her brows rising.

"He's a bright boy," Cecile insisted. "I've taught him some Latin, how to read and write, a little geography, and quite a bit of mathematics—"

"Mathematics? Goodness." The nun paused in her picking to rub a temple. "A devilishly difficult discipline. I get the worst headaches trying to deal with the convent's accounts. Who taught you that?"

"Sister Helene, back in my orphanage in Paris. She saw me fiddling with multiplication one day and set out to teach me more."

"An unusual education"—the nun glanced over Cecile's yellow dress, and the kerchief around her shoulders twined with embroidered vines—"for any King's Girl—even for a *bijou*, if I'm guessing correctly."

Ah, so she finally noticed. Cecile dropped her gaze for modesty's sake, but hope rippled through her. This conversation was going just as she'd planned. Cecile had worn her best dress in the hopes Mother Superior would recognize her as one of the better-educated of the King's Girls, a *bijou*. That could be worked to her advantage when Cecile asked for a second favor, a more outrageous one than a seat in a monastery school for Etienne.

The nun tossed a few more bean pods into the basket and put her empty hands on her hips. "Cecile, have you considered writing to your husband's family in France to see if they'll take in your stepson?"

She shook her head with more vehemence than was wise. "For reasons I've never really understood, my husband was disowned long before he came to these settlements." That was truth, but the real reason Cecile didn't write to France should be obvious to this nun. Etienne had been born *here*. He was a child of this land, where his mother's people and the people of other local tribes outnumbered the French by enormous numbers. She would never ship her darling off to a foreign place where he would never encounter another boy like himself—and pay the price of being different.

"Etienne is the son of my heart, Mother." She raised her chin. "I'm his only family now."

The nun nodded, brows drawn, and turned to weave her way deeper into the garden. Cecile followed, eyes on the low garden beds bursting with sorrel, yarrow not yet in flower, chamomile in seed, as well as parsley, chervil, and hyssop. The scent of mint rose up as she scuffed across some untamed vines. The nun paused only when they reached the far end of the garden, where a bramble of berry bushes glistened in the sun.

The nun finally said, with a sigh, "I must confess, Madame Tremblay, your request is a difficult one."

Cecile clutched the basket of beans close.

"This congregation of mine—" the nun waved a hand toward the main building "—has been controversial since I first founded it in that old stable at the edge of the woods. My sisters are not cloistered like nuns in every other convent. This has been…a point of contention between me, the bishop, and the local religious orders." The nun thrust an arm into a space in the blackberry thicket, heedless of thorns. "Because of the controversy, I fear I don't carry much influence with the Jesuits or the Franciscan *Récollets* who run the schools for boys in Montreal."

Cecile's spirits dipped.

"I suggest you pray very hard." The nun winced, elbow-deep in the brambles, as a thorn found its mark. "All I can do for you is to request, for your son, an interview with the brothers. After that, acceptance is up to Etienne."

"Oh, Mother." A weight tumbled off her shoulders. "I can ask no more than that. Thank you–"

"Thank me if I succeed," the Reverend Mother interrupted, "and only if I succeed." She pulled her arm from the brambles and held out a plump blackberry. "Try this, my dear. That maple candy failed to bring color back to your cheeks."

Cecile popped the berry in her mouth as tears came to her eyes, and not only because of the sharp-sour taste.

The nun laughed at her expression. "That's why wild blackberries of this country need to be baked with honey, in a pie or a crumble. They're so tart they make your eyes water. Now…" The nun plunged her arm back into the brambles. "We have a tentative plan for your son. But what of you, my dear? Will you hire yourself out? With your education, you're certainly qualified to be a governess, but there isn't much of a demand for that, even among the wealthiest merchants in Montreal."

Despite her elation for Etienne, a new worry scurried under Cecile's skin. She'd thought long and hard about this and had come to the conclusion that there was only one solution for her. A desperate solution that would allow her to stay close to Etienne and also offer sanctuary since, sooner or later—inevitably—her crimes would be found out.

"I have an idea, Mother," she said on the edge of a breath, "but it requires your approval."

"My dear," the nun said, "surely you've guessed by now that if it's within my power, I'm sure to grant your prayer."

"Very well." Cecile bent her head and forced out the words she had no choice but to speak. "I want to become a nun."

CHAPTER FIVE

On his first day at the building site, Theo set out to destroy the south wall of the chapel. With more joy than he'd put into any labor for years, he swung an iron-headed mallet until the impact of the hammer on the mortared stone shuddered up his arms and sent chips flying. As he pulled the mallet back, the mason who faced him swung at the same wall even harder. One of the erupting shards struck Theo just below the rolled-up sleeve of his mason's smock, scoring his forearm. Theo ignored the twinge and hurled the mallet around for another blow.

Yes, he'd picked the right angry laborer to help him destroy this section of the wall. The redheaded mason—by the name of Jules—was the man Theo had argued with nearly a fortnight ago, when the mason had risked Etienne's life with his negligence. So, when Theo had arrived this morning to announce himself as the new overseer, Theo wasn't surprised that the news set the mason seething. Jules might have hoped to get the overseer's position himself.

When another flying shard scored Theo's arm, Theo raised his gaze to meet the mason's blood-red glare. One flying shard was an accident. Two were a coincidence. If Theo got hit again, he'd have no choice but to toss down the mallet and make a lunge at Jules. First day on the job, Theo had to establish his skill and authority, but he'd rather not do either by violence. He needed every last worker if he were to raise the walls of this chapel, and he especially needed strong and experienced ones like this angry bull. Today, the two of them were either going to take this wall down together—or end up brawling amid half-shattered rock.

Fifty-fifty chance of the latter, Theo figured, pulling back for another swing.

"What are you *doing?*"

At the sound of the shout, Theo struck the wall with a wallop and then let the weight of the mallet bring down his arms. Standing just outside the radius of flying chips stood the fair-haired goddess he'd never expected to see again, glowing like a sunburst.

What the hell was *she* doing here? The only women supposed to be on these grounds were the nuns.

"Monsieur Martin." Her nostrils flared. "Mother Superior hired you to *build* a chapel."

"And that is—" he gripped the mallet with two hands, ready to swing anew "—what I'm doing."

"You are standing in a pile of rubble."

"You shouldn't be here, woman." Jules wiped an arm across his forehead as he squinted beneath it. "Haven't you learned—"

"Jules is right," Theo interrupted in a voice fierce enough to shut the mason up. "This is a dangerous place. And we've got work to do."

"I admire your industriousness," she said in a way that didn't at all sound like admiration, "but the Reverend Mother has made it my responsibility to keep an eye on the progress of the building."

Like hell she did.

He didn't say the words out loud but she twitched and took a halting step back as if she'd heard them.

"She hired *me* as the overseer." Theo planted the mallet head on the ground and gripped the tip of the handle. "I'll be the one telling the Reverend Mother what she needs to know."

Movement out of the corner of his eye proved to be Etienne, striding toward his mother from where Theo had assigned him to tend the fires of the lime ricks. The half-grown boy stopped a few feet away from his mother, shooting Theo a frown like a warning.

The boy muttered, "What are you doing here, Mother?"

"I'm not here to bother you, Etienne." She looked over the boy's smock, dusted with ash. "I've already agreed to let you work here, so long as you remember your promise. After you're done laboring, you must study for the monastery exam."

"I will," Etienne said, throwing out his arms to take in the building site and all the men watching. "But you shouldn't be here."

His mother tilted her head, face softening, giving the boy a look that pulsed with affection. Behind Theo's sternum, something yanked. He'd lived over two and a half decades, yet his years of indentured service had stolen away all memory of such gentleness.

I will get it back.

All of it.

"My business is with Monsieur Martin," she said softly. "You mustn't worry. It won't take long."

"Well, if it's about the wall, the overseer is right." Etienne eyed every man within sight and didn't skip over Theo. "There were too many stones mortared against the grain."

"That may be true," she said, turning her attention back to Theo. "But before the Reverend Mother left this morning, she didn't say a thing to me about destroying a wall."

"Because the Reverend Mother deferred all construction decisions to *me*." Theo resisted the urge to drink in the beauty of her, in her yellow dress, battered leather boots peeking out from the frothy hem. By the look darkening her son's face, Theo was failing. "And," he added, "when she left this morning, the Reverend Mother didn't mention your involvement."

A sigh lifted her chest in a way he shouldn't be noticing. Etienne hadn't budged from her side. Realizing—as Etienne had—that all the workers had paused in their labors to watch the drama unfolding, Theo handed his mallet to the nearest mason and directed the woman toward a table under a canopy away from the dust and building debris.

"Let's talk privately." He nodded briefly at her son, admiring the boy's protectiveness even if it was against him. "You, Etienne, get back to work."

Madame Tremblay swiveled on a heel to walk toward a canvas canopy beneath which he kept the chapel plans and supply lists, pinned to a table by rocks. To the sound of Jules's deep-throated laughter, Theo followed her, watching how her blonde hair, gathered in a roll at her nape, brushed her neck as she wove around piles of fieldstone. With every step, her skirts shifted across her nicely rounded backside in a way that made every man's attention sharpen—until his glare joined Etienne's, and they all turned back to work.

When she reached the table, she headed straight to the far side. He ducked his head under the shelter to join her, stopping inside the cool shade. Crossing his arms, he braced himself for…for what? She was a slip of a girl.

She held no power over him.

"I spoke to the Reverend Mother this morning," he began, "as she was climbing into the canoe to go to Quebec. She agreed to the terms of my employment and told me to start today as overseer."

The lady lifted her pretty chin. "I spoke to her, too, before she left the convent with her satchel. She made no mention of me at all?"

"Not a word."

She tented her fingertips on the table and leaned into them. "It is becoming clear that though Sister Martha is a holy woman capable of persuading bishops and kings to bend to her will, when it comes to smaller matters, she relies on blind faith and grand assumptions."

He couldn't make any sense out of that muttering, so he stood and breathed in the scent of cut grass and violets coming off her. The fragrance muddled his senses in a way that it shouldn't, for a man who'd be on his way home to France in ten weeks and one day.

"Why," he said, harsher than he meant to, "are you still here at the congregation and not with your husband?"

Her head swept up, brown eyes flashing, but her attention rested on him for only a moment—like a bird alighting upon a branch—before darting away. Her flitting unease brought to his attention the fact that he was head-and-shoulders taller than her, sweaty, breathing hard, covered in stone dust, and bursting with frustration at this delay. He uncrossed his arms in an effort to look less intimidating.

"Sister Martha—the Reverend Mother," she said, keeping her gaze low, "has agreed to take me into the convent as a laywoman, until she gets back from Quebec. As for my husband…he has disappeared into the wilderness. I'm…I have reason to believe I'm widowed."

A rush of something went through him, blowing away the phantom husband he'd imagined at her back. To think this lovely woman might be unclaimed by any man.

"Sister Martha," she forged on, "has taken me in on a provisional basis, in the same way she has hired you. She has tasked me with two duties—first, to reconcile the convent accounts that have been neglected in her two-year absence, and two, to keep a daily journal of the work accomplished, and expenses spent, on the building until she returns."

He dragged hot air deep into his lungs, the acrid ash of the nearby lime ricks searing the lining of his windpipe. This utter lack of respect…. He should be used to it by now. "The Reverend Mother," he said, "doesn't trust me."

"She doesn't *know* you. Or me, for that matter. We're both strangers she took in on faith." She crossed her arms. "But I'm here as a volunteer, paid only with meals and a pallet. Her expectations for you are higher, since your wages are costing the congregation dearly."

Theo suppressed a flinch. Only his master benefited from those outrageous wages. Making the congregation pay was the only way the bastard would give up his favorite slab of muscle. Theo would have worked on this building site for free, after so many years of hauling out stumps. But an indentured servant had no control over his world.

Suddenly, he couldn't bear to stand here any longer like a servant in her ladylike presence.

"If we're done"—he took a step into the sun—"I've got work to do."

"Not yet." She stopped him with a tense but quivering voice. "I admit I am completely ignorant of building matters. Yet I find myself tasked with the responsibility of making sense of such matters in a journal that will be read by Sister Martha when she returns. To that end… Would you explain to me, in a way that I can understand, why you must destroy that wall?"

He opened his mouth, ready to give her an earful, for he'd built a chateau in Maincy for one of the Sun King's ministers, he'd built the Church of Saint-Roch in Paris, and he'd had a hand in enlarging the Palace of Versailles. But when he faced her, he ran into a chin raised in pride, cheeks pale as clouds, and a trembling mouth.

She was terrified of something—could it be *him?* He could all but see the fear pulsing under that fair skin. What the hell was he doing, terrifying this woman? He uncurled the fists he'd made at his sides.

"Let me ask you a question." He drew in a deep breath and forced himself to be calm. "Do you want this chapel to stand for a thousand years?"

"Of course." She swallowed so hard he saw the flex of her throat. "Though the Reverend Mother may agree that five hundred years would do—if it means the work could proceed more quickly and with some savings."

"If a wall can be shattered as easily as we are shattering that one," he said, tilting his head toward where the crash of mallets continued, "you won't get *five* years out of this building."

A pulse jumped in her jaw. Seeing it made him want to touch it.

With his tongue.

Damn, he needed a night in a tavern.

"Surely," she said in a low voice, "there's a better way to fix it than knocking the whole thing down."

"There is only one way to build a stone building, and that's the *right* way." He held up a hand before she could protest. "The problem is just as your son said. The wall is riddled with stones mortared against the grain."

Her forehead rippled. "How did this happen?"

"One—or more—of the masons are careless or inexperienced. I don't know who yet." Theo suspected several might not be masons at all, but they had claimed they were in order to secure the higher wage. "I don't know who mortared that part of the wall, but when I find out, I will teach them that every stone has to resist the pressure of the stones above. One ill-laid stone weakens the entire building."

"Such a small thing…"

"Not a small thing at all." He planted his hands on his hips, squinting at the building site. He glimpsed her son pacing by the lime ricks, agitated and frowning, squinting across the distance at him and his mother talking under the canopy.

"Imagine, Madame Tremblay, if we kept that wall the way it is, and then it collapsed without warning. On a gathered congregation—or on your son."

"Your point is made, sir." She clutched her own arms and ran her hands from shoulder to elbow. "Tell me this, then: How long will destroying this wall delay the completion of the project?"

"Impossible to say."

"Sister Martha told me she wants the roof to be installed by Christmas."

"She'd better pray hard." He pulled up the hem of his smock and wiped his brow with it, an excuse not to witness the lady's surging distress. "When the weather gets bad, and the temperature drops, the water in mortar freezes. It won't bond to stone. You can't do masonry when the temperature drops too low. And even the best of carpenters can't put a roof on unfinished walls."

She uncrossed her arms and planted them on her hips instead. "You're saying the work stops in…October?"

"Earlier if September winds bring a chill. And it won't start up again until April."

"Then why is Sister Martha under the impression that it'll only take a few months more to finish?"

He couldn't help himself, remembering her own words. "Perhaps she relies too much on blind faith and grand assumptions."

She raised those lovely lashes, acknowledging the homage, though her gaze was still wary. "Nonetheless," she said, "Sister Martha is still relying on you—on *us*—to help her fulfill the promises she has made to her superiors. Surely there is some way we can avoid disappointing her."

The gut-kick to reassure this lovely woman was almost too much to bear. *Don't worry, I will get the best from these men. We'll be mortaring at all hours and raising walls faster than you can imagine…*

He would, indeed, be getting the best from these men, but they faced an impossible deadline. He thought hard, watching as she shuffled her weight from one foot to the other, thinking even harder.

As intelligent, he thought, as she was beautiful.

He shunted the dangerous thought away.

"I'm out of my depth, monsieur." She stepped away from the long table and into the sun, heading toward the main convent building. "I'll have to ponder this for a while. I thank you for being forthright."

"Wait." Why couldn't he keep his mouth shut? "There may be one thing we can do."

Having stepped into the bright sun, she twisted with a swirl of skirts, stilling like a saint in the frescoes of the Church of Saint-Roch. A stroke of yellow against jewel-green grass. Beyond her blurred the slate-gray of the Saint Lawrence River, the pine green of fir trees, and the cloud-studded sky.

"We'd get the work done faster," he said through a throat gone tight, "if we had more laborers."

"Skilled masons are impossible to find, as you well know. And more laborers would drain the building budget."

"Not if we find young, inexperienced ones we can use as apprentices. They can mind the lime ricks and stir the mortar, like your son. That would free up the older boys, and I could teach them to work with stone."

She canted her head. "But how to find those laborers? As it stands, most able-bodied men are already heading out into the wilderness for the fur-trapping season. The laborers left behind are clearing land on seigneuries all up and down the river. And the budget—"

"Trust me, I will find laborers who will work hard and cheap and I won't miss a day of work. By the time I can gather them, the Reverend Mother will be back, so she can make the hiring decision. The matter will be out of your hands."

"It won't be. You're mistaken." She shaded her eyes so she didn't have to squint. "The budget is a vexing matter, but I hope to be in charge of it for a very long time. I may be a laywoman now, Monsieur Martin, but as soon as this matter of my missing husband is settled, I intend to join this congregation as a nun."

He smiled before he could stop himself.

"Sir." She stiffened. "Do you doubt me?"

"Madame, I wouldn't dare."

"I'm not jesting, you know."

He had enough sense to hold his tongue. But this spectacularly beautiful woman, taking vows? A ludicrous idea. He tried to imagine a wimple covering that lovely throat and a dull gray dress dimming the brilliance of her. Yes, he'd gleaned from their short acquaintance that she was uncomfortable among his laborers and terrified of him. Indeed, how could he blame such a beauty for keeping her guard up in such rough settlements? Were she to walk through Montreal in that dress, she'd cause a riot.

He supposed threatening to join a convent was as good a way as any to keep men at bay. That must be why she was saying such a ridiculous thing, to keep him—and others—at arm's length.

He bowed to her ruse and said, "I hear you, Madame Tremblay. May you succeed in your efforts."

With a swirl of skirts, she turned on a heel and strode back toward the main building of the convent with a back as straight as a white pine.

He watched every lovely, twitching step.

This woman taking vows?

He didn't believe it for a minute.

CHAPTER SIX

A fortnight later, Cecile stood outdoors by the stable amid the violet gloaming of a fading day. She slid her gaze from five potential laborers toward the vexing man who'd gathered them. Her glare had no effect on the grinning overseer, who let his long, strong body fall back against the log wall. He kicked the sole of one foot against it and crossed his stone-dusted arms in a way that made his muscles bulge. Worst of all, he eyed her with the same expression of amusement as when she'd first announced to him that she intended to become a nun.

Annoyance rippled through her. That comment had been meant to put him off—not pique his curiosity or interest. And yet his eyes glinted in a way that unnerved her more than usual. He couldn't be serious about hiring these half-starved youths to work at the building site. Had he just used them to lure her out of the convent and across a field to the old stable, where he could dismiss these so-called laborers and thus be alone in the dusk to tweak her terrors?

Saints alive, the world was full of wolves.

"Monsieur Martin." She jerked her chin toward the ragged group gathered around an outdoor fire. "You must be joking, bringing this crew to me. These are not working men."

"They are," he said, his voice light. "They are too young to go trading and too skinny to pull tree stumps and clear land. But I've convinced them to give honest work on a building site a try."

A more motley group of ragamuffins she'd never seen. "They're barely out of childhood."

"François"—He jerked his chin toward the gangly boy supervising the others around the cooking fire—"is seventeen."

Thin as a bean, François looked years younger than Etienne, who was just fourteen. "I assume the other children are all younger?"

"In age, yes, but not in life experience." He shrugged those massive shoulders, which she'd seen brazenly bare and gleaming as he worked shirtless in the hot August sun, damn him. "These young men will strive harder than half the crew already laboring on that building site. I would wager my pay on it, if I could."

She wished she *could* claw back some of the overseer's outrageous wages. The Reverend Mother— who preferred to be called Sister Martha—was extraordinarily good at soliciting donations, but she refused to bargain with vendors and was hopeless at keeping track of expenses. While looking over the accounts, Cecile had already discovered that the butcher in Montreal regularly overcharged by an order of magnitude. And all the hired masons were richly compensated, though none as much as this man. A man she still couldn't believe was an indentured servant. He looked like the *least* likely kind of man to suffer an existence under another man's thumb.

As her stomach started to churn, she tore her attention away from the fingers tapping against his swelling bicep and focused on the matter at hand, a tactic she'd used often since they'd started working together. "I knew laborers would be scarce. But I expected, over the last few weeks, you would gather adults, maybe refugees in need of work."

"There's peace with the Iroquois, so there are not as many Huron refugees as in previous years." That vexing smile widened, softening his hard-planed features. "If you prefer, I know some drunks I might be able to coax out of the tavern—"

"Don't be absurd."

"—or I could fetch prisoners from the fort. But I can't vouch for their work ethic, or their physical condition, after spending time in that jail."

A trickle slid down her spine. She'd once met a man—a friend of her husband's—who'd spent some time in that Montreal jail. He liked to plant a mangled leg on a chair and boast of how he'd survived the notorious "boot." Prison guards had affixed two planks around his calf, from ankle to knee, and wedges had been pounded ever deeper between the planks and his leg until he confessed…or his leg snapped.

Thank heavens, she thought with a shiver, that she and Etienne had attained a measure of sanctuary from the law.

"Madame"—the overseer pushed away from the wall and stood on spread feet—"if I'd seen any hale and hearty men between the ages of twenty and fifty, I would have offered them the opportunity to work here. But they would have cost you much more than this crew. All these young workers need are room, food, and safety. That's a treasure beyond imagining for them."

She gave the children a keener assessment, shifting her attention to a boy whose coloring suggested he was a full-blooded Huron. Against an ill-fitting shirt, ribs showed on the boy's narrow chest. She glanced at a smaller boy, who stood next to the gangly François. Bony-kneed, dirty-faced, wearing breeches too short for his legs and a shirt that looked like it hadn't been laundered all season. With a heart-pull, she was reminded of the first time she'd laid eyes upon her stepson, right down to the unkempt hair hanging in his eyes.

This wretched, unsettling overseer had done this on purpose. He must have figured that she—a mother herself—would look upon this woebegone collection of unloved waifs and her heart would overrule all doubts. The churning in her gut could just be the old fears rising, but it could also prove his tactics to appeal to her softer side were working.

But the mason hadn't taken into account that every financial decision she made would be scrutinized by Sister Martha. Cecile figured that employing the older boy, François, would be acceptable—after all, it had been the Reverend Mother's suggestion to give Etienne a position among the workers to keep him out of trouble until she could make arrangements for his schooling. But as for setting the smaller, half-starved children to labor for their bread… Wouldn't the nun be more inclined to see them settled in easier circumstances, somewhere other than laboring at a building site?

She gathered as much air as she could muster. "Monsieur Martin—"

"Theo," he retorted.

She blinked, knocked back by his vehemence.

"Theo," he repeated, hiking his hands on his hips, where the waistband of his breeches sagged. "I'm no 'monsieur,' not until I'm a free man again. Just like you're not Sister Anything until you take vows."

She stilled, her ribs tightening. She couldn't possibly call him Theo. There was intimacy in speaking someone's first name, and intimacy with men was exactly what she'd come to the convent to avoid. Bad enough that she had to see this disturbing mason every day. He looked like a brute, stood like a soldier, and worked alongside the other laborers until he was just as drenched in sweat. Whenever he loomed into her presence, her gut flexed between terror, resistance, and some other prickly feeling she feared examining too closely.

"Call me Theo," he said more softly, before pointing at the misfits around the fire. "And call them François, Pierre, Michel, Jacques, and Jean—"

"Sister Martha," she interrupted, as a breeze tossed the needle-heavy boughs of the pines nearby, "will accept François and perhaps Michel as workers. But as for the other children—"

"She wants the building done above all else, doesn't she?"

Cecile huffed a breath. "Of course, but—"

"I'll be teaching these boys a trade, and they'll help me finish the building sooner. And isn't caring for the poor the work of a nun, as well, Madame Tremblay, soon-to-be Sister…Sister what? Have you picked a saint's name yet?"

Sometimes courage was foolhardy—but this man's overbearing confidence prompted her to shoot him an angry gaze. Wasn't he full of questions about things he had no business knowing and she didn't dare divulge?

Stay focused on the children. She jerked a chin at the crowd. "Where did you find them?"

"On the streets of Montreal. Hungry, without a home or family. In physical danger."

All five kids stood still, watching her and Theo—no, Monsieur Martin. Their eyes gleamed in the firelight and she fell into those gazes one by one, a soreness growing in her chest. *Dear heavens.*

Tearing her gaze away, she let her head fall back and blinked at the sky. Dusk had turned to twilight, for the stars above winked. The scented smoke of roasting meat wafted above her, rising from two skinned rabbits turning on a wooden spit. In her mind was burned the sight of the group, especially the youngest, who didn't look older than ten. Cecile wasn't even sure the waif wasn't a girl, dressed as a boy for her own protection.

What would happen to a young girl left alone on the streets of Montreal?

"Before I started working here," Theo began, his voice much gentler than it had been moments ago. "I used to come to Montreal about once a month to fetch supplies and do an odd job or two when there was opportunity. One of those boys picked my pocket. I followed, got back what he stole, but Jacques slipped away. Every return trip, I noticed them more, skulking around corners, stealing food from carts, avoiding me. François had carved loaded dice to entice fools to gamble. He fed the rest of the group on those wages until he tried to trick the wrong man and was beaten bloody." A muscle flexed in his cheek. "What you're looking at are powder boys escaped from French ships, the bastard children of deceased tavern women, and *Métis* still unsure where they belong in this world."

His voice slid into her ear, rough in the way fur could be, when scuffed backward. This unlikely savior had apparently been watching out for these young thieves for some time. She couldn't help herself—she looked at Theo, *really* looked at him. In profile, his jaw had gone tense, and his lowered brows cast his eyes in shadows. Baffling, how gentleness could thrive in a confounding man of such burly, commanding strength.

You're a puzzle, Theo Martin.

"If you agree to house them here," he said, forging on into the silence, "I promise to give them light work. Then I can shift other laborers to more skilled work, like laying stone."

Cecile heard footsteps just as Etienne strode out of the darkness, passing by her with a load of firewood in his arms. She turned and lifted her hand, intending to ruffle his midnight-black hair as he passed, but she stilled as she glimpsed a hard look in his eyes. A warning burned in those black depths, directed past her toward Theo, who, she realized, had sidled close to her—too close for Etienne's comfort, it seemed.

Ah, my son, she thought, taking a reflexive sidestep away. *You cannot protect me from every man who looks my way.*

Etienne continued his pace toward the open fire, his shoulders straight. As the boy stoked the fire, he raised his gaze above the flames, watching the two of them—watching Theo, really—with a wary glare. Goodness, when did Etienne's flippant gratitude for being saved by Theo switch to suspicion? Yes, she and the overseer had been spending an uneasy hour together every morning, but the mason had made no untoward move or statement, other than teasing her about becoming a nun. She supposed Etienne couldn't help himself, having been raised in such a dangerous household. He was still the boy determined to protect her against all threats, real or imagined.

In truth, the only thing she needed protection against right now was the forcefulness of Theo's arguments.

In that, she admitted defeat.

"When Sister Martha returns," she murmured into the darkness, "I'd appreciate your help in explaining the presence of laboring children."

He made a noise, a low sucking of air between his teeth. "You'll take them in?"

"Of course I will." She frowned. "Do you think I'm a monster?"

He flashed a white-toothed grin that she quickly turned away from, losing her breath altogether.

"Perhaps," she found herself saying, words rising in spite of her better sense, "the youngest among them"—*the girl*—"shouldn't labor on the building site, but instead set traps for small game, or hunt. I assume that bow and arrow belong to Jean?"

Jeanne?

From the side of her eye, she saw him nod.

"There are plenty of porcupines and rabbits in these woods," she continued, though her voice had gone high. "I assume Jean knows how to set a trap. Eel season is coming, and wild berries need picking. Earning one's keep can be done not just by physical labor, but also by adding to the communal larder." *Why am I babbling?* "There's no room in the crew's bunkhouse, so they'll have to sleep here, in the old stable. I'll arrange for pallets. We might have to fix the roof—"

"I'll see it done."

"Very well." She hugged her arms not because it was cold—it was decidedly *not*—but because she could feel herself unraveling. "I'll come to the stable in the evenings after dinner, while there's still light, to teach them to read." After all, while trying to entice Sister Martha to let her take vows, she'd told the nun that she could be a teacher for the convent school. Wouldn't this be a fine way to prove her skills? "I'll borrow slates from the school and primers—"

"You have a good heart, Madame Tremblay."

That voice seeped through the cracks in her control. She forced her spine into an iron rod. "I'd better have a good heart," she retorted, "since I intend to become a nun."

He rumbled a low laugh that left no doubt that his skepticism hadn't waned. In truth, she didn't *want* to be a nun—that was a tactic to protect against the long reach of the law. She couldn't tell him that, so how was she to explain her choice? And why did she feel like she should? Was it the violet shadows of the deepening evening, or the music of the breeze dancing in the pines, or the fragrance of honeysuckle drifting over the field? No, no—such things no longer held any power over her. She wasn't a foolish young girl anymore. Yet somehow, tonight, Theo had dragged up a yearning to have, for her own, the same kind of care and protection that this man, at great effort, now offered these orphans.

He murmured, "You've done a fine thing today. I am in your debt, Madame Tremblay."

"Cecile."

The name slipped out before she could stop it, before she could even think of taking it back, before she could chide herself for being addled.

"I suppose," she breathed, "it's futile to stick to formality now. After all, we've just become co-conspirators...Theo."

CHAPTER SEVEN

With the sun beating on his head and six feet up on a scaffold, Theo thrust his trowel into a bucket of mortar, which gave way to the blade like thickened cream. He pulled up a dollop and smeared the mortar across the top of the uneven wall, making sure it filled every gap. The backs of his hands burned in spots from drying smears, but Theo didn't mind. Soon, his hands would be hardened against the caustic filling. Feeling that pinching sensation brought back the years of his apprenticeship, when he was a soft-handed boy first working the mortar in the shadow of a rising cathedral, feeling like he was stirring up the very stuff that held the world together.

Before his world exploded.

A throaty woman's voice rose among the babble of working men. He didn't have to look down to know to whom it belonged. Steady in timbre, firm in tone, with a husky undercurrent that gave promise to softness. The sound vibrated in his ears and amplified throughout his body, rippling in dangerous places. He focused on spreading the mortar while bracing for her to throw a bolt of lightning by calling him by his first name again.

Jules's voice joined hers and Theo's mood hardened like the mortar under his trowel. He couldn't pick out the conversation, but by the jocular lift in the other man's voice, Theo knew the mason was flirting in his swaggering way. His grip tightened. That arrogant redhead had been a thorn in his side from the first, a boastful, skilled worker too easily distracted by the pretty novices hanging laundry outside the convent schoolhouse.

And now, by Cecile.

Theo set a stone on the spread mortar and turned, squinting against the blaze of the August sun. Below, Jules stood right in front of Cecile, dangerously close. He must have stepped into her path, for she tended to walk wide circles with her head down around any gathered masons. She now held her ground but leaned back, the cords in her neck tight.

Afraid.

Realization struck him hard. Some man, at some point in her life, had physically hurt this lovely woman. He'd suspected since he'd first noticed the scar at her temple that she tried to hide. The fact that she'd been abused kicked up a whole barrage of questions, as well as a burn in his belly. Right now, it made him keenly aware of Jules standing too close, gripping Cecile's willowy waist.

"Jules!" he barked, biting back the surging, ridiculous words *hands off my woman* as he clanked the trowel upon the wall. "Get back to work."

Jules didn't flinch—or look up—but his swaggering smile stretched. Cecile's gaze slid up to Theo's. Through a vein of red fury, Theo read a plea in those fathomless eyes.

He leapt off the scaffolding, hitting the ground hard. Straightening to his full height, he glared at the dirty, hairy-knuckled hand splayed upon Cecile's waist. Gripped by the urge to seize the mason by the scruff and launch him bodily against the wall they were building, he took a few strides until the stink of Jules's sweat filled his nose.

"You have work to do." Grabbing a handful of the fool's smock, Theo yanked him away from Cecile and then pulled him around so they stood nose-to-nose. "Get back to it."

Jules's bloodshot eyes shot flames. "I'll get back to it when I damn well please."

Though Theo's hard-earned survival lessons screamed *Mind your business, keep your head down, don't start any trouble*, his fist had its own mind. It headed toward Jules's jaw with a blow that sent the mason reeling. The punch having landed, Theo shook his hand, bones aching, as Jules tumbled over a wheelbarrow and fell hard on his tailbone.

Damn, Theo should have known better, and yet, hadn't this confrontation been inevitable? Hadn't the antagonism been building between them since the first day they'd met?

Didn't a lady like Cecile deserve to be protected from grabby, greedy fools?

It took the sprawled mason a few seconds, but he came to his feet enraged. Jules's fist aimed for Theo's jaw but Theo anticipated it. He turned so his shoulder took the impact. Recovering, he lunged, throwing his weight into the mason's gut, forcing the air out of Jules's lungs and driving the fool to the ground. Theo straddled him and struck several blows. Dust billowed up as Jules bucked free his legs, clamped them around one of Theo's thighs, and rolled Theo over in a move that would have impressed Theo, if he weren't the one who'd lost the upper hand.

Jules's shadow loomed over him, his arm raised. Theo took a punch and returned two, then lurched up to throw off his opponent. The mason tumbled to the side and hit the dirt hard.

Theo surged to his feet and stood over the mason, fists ready. Jules raised his arms, palms open, then coughed blood-strewn spittle onto the ground.

When Theo saw the blood, his better sense resurged. Beating Jules to a pulp would feel *damn good*, but he had his position as an indentured servant and overseer to consider—and his workers were watching the melee with sharp eyes.

This had to end now.

"The only thing in your hands should be a trowel and a bucket," Theo barked, straightening as he loosened his fists. "Keep your hands off her."

Through squinting eyes, Jules looked from him to Cecile and then back to him, setting loose a laugh that launched more streaked spittle. Cecile hadn't moved an inch, Theo noticed, except to go pale and shrink into herself. He realized he must look like a monster to her, covered in stone dust, streaked with blood.

Stepping away from Jules, Theo strode toward Cecile. Her eyes widened as she took a shaky step back.

He stopped in his tracks. "I apologize for my insolent worker." He wanted to add, *Cecile*, the name lurching to his mouth, but he forced himself to choose formality since every man on the site was watching. "That won't happen again."

She straightened a few inches, laboring to relax her terrified expression into a stony mask he knew too well. And yet he'd caught her off guard in inky twilight the other night, when she'd gazed at the children he'd brought in for laborers. Her eyes, many shades of brown and black, had swirled with feelings she'd held in check.

"I...I thank you, sir." She lowered her voice and her gaze. "It seems you have a habit of intervening in other people's trouble."

More than you will ever know. "That mason will keep hands to himself from now on," he promised. "I'll see to it."

Her lashes fluttered as her attention shifted to his jaw. "You're bleeding."

"It's nothing." He swiped his mouth.

She frowned and looked over at Jules, still on the ground, head down, arms slung over his knees. "Should I tend to—"

"No." He imagined Cecile taking care of the mason, and Jules in his brutish rebellion reaching around and probing the soft curves of her backside. Theo would have to punch the man a lot harder—and maybe punch himself, too, for wishing *he* was holding her like that.

He forced the thought away. "That man—" he flung a hand toward Jules "—has taken worse beatings. He'll be fine. Is there a matter you wanted to discuss with me?"

"No.… I just came by to see how Etienne is doing." She blew air out between her lips, the breeze making a slip of silken tress fly up. "I've been neglecting him."

"He's probably in the woods. I sent him to collect firewood for the lime ricks." It hadn't passed Theo's notice that Etienne was most sullen just after Theo's morning conference with his mother. Theo preferred to send the boy away to brood in private, rather than yell at him. "It's good your son wasn't here," he added. "He'd have come to your rescue, and

Jules would not have spared him because of his youth."

"I appreciate you keeping Etienne out of such melees." She frowned. "Perhaps, going forward, I'll stay away from the site altogether."

"If you'd like. But you didn't start this, and most of my men know their manners. As for the tussle between us…" He gestured to Jules, still sitting, slapping the dust from his mason's smock. "That was a long time coming."

"The blood on both your faces suggests it was more than a tussle."

"The fight is over. Watch."

He swiveled on a heel and took a few steps until he towered over Jules. "No more work for you today."

Jules leaned back on his hands and squinted up, one eye swelling fast. "Are you firing me, Monsieur Overseer?"

Theo frowned. "Are you going to bother the women anymore?"

"Yeah," Jules retorted, giving him a bloody smile. "Just not the ones around here."

Damn fool. Pushing his luck, even in defeat. Theo recognized the type. Back in France, when he'd finally become a master mason, he'd had to discipline more than one young apprentice. This Jules was like a wolf pup—he needed to feel teeth in his neck before he'd fall back in with the rest of the pack.

"How badly you behave when you're not in my sight," Theo said to the grinning mason, "is someone else's fight. Now stand up."

Theo thrust out his hand, urging Jules to take it. Jules eyed the outstretched arm, tilted his head, and took a long time to think about it. Theo was about to pull his arm back when Jules seized Theo's forearm.

With a lunge, the mason was on his feet. The flames in his eyes had dimmed, but his gaze still danced with bravado.

Jules tapped his swollen eye. "Nice right hook you got there, Overseer."

Theo accepted the backhanded compliment and met it in kind. "That leg twist of yours knocked the breath out of me."

"Learned it in the back alleys of a port town in Brittany." Jules tested his jaw in the cup of his hand. "Where'd you learn how to fight? Was it in the streets of Guéret…or during your time in prison?"

CHAPTER EIGHT

*P*rison.

Sitting in the bow of a canoe now cutting a wake through the Saint Lawrence River, Cecile squeezed her eyes shut as the word *prison* clanged a sonorous bell in her head. That alarm joined all the other discordant bells echoing through her mind since she'd marched away from Theo in the aftermath of the fistfight two days ago. Unfortunately, shutting herself up in the convent to avoid interactions with Theo, and pressing a pillow over her ears, hadn't helped her forget what she'd heard. Or the violence she'd witnessed. Now, even the wobble of the canoe made those bells clang louder.

Theo Martin, criminal.

Up surged the old fear, the acid cold, the softening of tendons, the trip-flutter of her pulse. Lifting her legs, she twisted on the bench to face

Etienne, paddling in the stern. Focusing on her stubble-chinned son always helped ease her tumbling panic—she never wanted Etienne to witness that. Not for the first time today, she noticed that her son's once boyishly narrow shoulders had begun to strain the seams of his linen shirt. He'd been working hard on that building site, pushing wheelbarrows full of stone, stirring slowly hardening vats of mortar, building some muscle under the eyes of Theo—

Theo the *fighter*.

The spinning panic grew spikes. She sat straight up, wobbling the vessel.

Etienne shot her a glance. "Were you dozing, Mother?"

"No, no. I was… startled by a dragonfly." It seemed a good enough excuse. Dozens of them hovered, iridescent wings vibrating, by the reeds near the riverbank.

Etienne laughed, a low, manly rumble that bore no resemblance to the childlike giggle she feared she would never hear again. "They don't bite," he said. "And we're moving too fast for them to land on you anyway. We're almost at the convent."

So soon? She dug her teeth into her lower lip. All morning, during a picnic excursion to the picturesque Lachine Rapids just upstream from Montreal, she'd been seeking a moment to broach the subject of Theo with Etienne, to see if he'd heard anything about Theo's criminal history. But two issues deterred her. First, Etienne was always bearish and moody when she spoke about Theo, and second, justice and punishment were fraught subjects between them because of all the measures she was taking to dodge their own entanglement with the law. They'd shared a whole long morning together, and she'd never quite found her tongue.

"You're wearing yourself out paddling," she said, frustrated. "Can you slow down a little?"

And stop growing up?

"I couldn't slow down even if I wanted to." Etienne shrugged, the dappled sun dancing silver over his shiny black hair. "The current is running fast."

Everything was running fast. The water, her warring thoughts…and time. She peeled her hands from the gunwales and set them on the blanket folded on her lap. This matter of Theo's criminal past, maybe *violent* past, could affect Etienne, who worked closely with him every day. If only she could make sense of it all. Yes, Theo had been convicted of a crime he'd hidden from her. She was running away from her own crime, so who was she to judge? Yet Theo was *also* capable of great violence—and the combination churned her stomach.

Etienne's sudden laugh jerked her back to attention. Sunlight glanced over her eyes, blinding as the canoe rounded a jutting outcropping to come within sight of the congregations' landing place.

"Mother," Etienne said in a voice compressed with humor, "you may want to avert your eyes."

"Whyever for—oh!"

She turned her head away so fast that the roll of hair at the nape of her neck swung to brush a shoulder. She'd averted her eyes too late, though, to avoid seeing a group of naked men, splashing around knee-deep in the river. How had she forgotten that every Sunday, in good weather, the laborers bathed on the banks of the Saint Lawrence?

Now behind her eyes was branded the picture of a great variety of hairy naked men's bodies.

She could tell by the laughter and mocking hailing that they'd seen her, too. "Goodness," she said. "I know the nuns shut themselves in the convent during their bathing time, but don't the workers realize they're only a long stone's throw from the windows?"

"Yeah," Etienne said, his voice cracking more from suppressed laughter than the ongoing changing of his voice. "They just don't care."

"Head farther downstream, Etienne, and fast." Witnessing her son's snickering and shaking shoulders reminded her that, yes, he was still a boy—if only in the way all men were boys. "We'll disembark farther downstream."

The current pulled hard on the keel, shooting them downriver. Soon after, Etienne staked his paddle hard into the water to veer the bow of the canoe toward the bank at the far east edge of the landholding. Pulling up to the steeper bank, Etienne jumped onto the water's edge and yanked the canoe onto the hard-packed verge. She folded the blanket over her arm and took Etienne's hand as he helped her out. Only when she reached the top of the bluff did she dare a brief glance toward the faraway bathers and was distracted by the sight of someone swimming deeper into the river.

The man's head bobbed out of the water long enough for her to recognize with a jolt the dark-haired, clean-shaven man who'd taken unwelcome root in her thoughts.

"Etienne, why is Monsieur Martin out there?" She didn't dare call him Theo in front of her son.

"I dunno." He made a grunting noise. "Probably showing off by fighting the current."

She squinted, ignoring Etienne's scowl. "He's taking something off that floating log."

Etienne joined her at the top of the bluff as she watched Theo shift a small burden to his other arm, keeping whatever it was above the water level before slinging his free arm over the timber. The floating log carried Theo and his burden downstream, and when the tree trunk started drifting farther from the shore and into a swifter midriver current, Theo released his grip and swam toward the riverbank. Awkwardly, he labored toward where Etienne had pulled up their canoe. As he entered the shallows, he found the river bottom and then rose to his full height.

She didn't realize she'd been holding her breath until dizziness made her sway on her feet. Theo wasn't naked like the other bathing men, but his long linen shirt clung to his body from throat to just above his knees. His sleeves were rolled up above carved forearms, and the moisture-translucent linen pasted to his shoulders, the planes of his chest, the ripples of his abdomen—and where he was wearing a low-slung loincloth beneath—where she *shouldn't be staring.* Forcing her spine into a rod, she swiveled away, pretending to find interest in the woods beyond.

Etienne raised his voice. "Is that what I think it is?"

"I saw it running up and down that timber."

Theo made his way up the bluff, she heard his squelching footsteps.

He said, "Want to hold it, Etienne?"

"Hold it?" Etienne shook his head. "Why did you bother saving it? I've been stabbed by those needles more than once."

"This one's quills are barely hardened," Theo said. By the length of his shadow, Cecile guessed that he'd reached the top of the berm. "You want to hold it, Cecile?"

She sensed, rather than saw, Etienne stiffen at Theo's casual use of her given name. Saints alive, didn't Theo know any better than to talk to her that way within her son's hearing? And why did Theo decide to swim back to shore *here*, when she'd been avoiding him for the last few days? This felt like an ambush and left her no choice—in spite of her swimming senses—but to pivot and face him.

She intended to focus on the black ball of a creature he held in the crook of his elbow, but the man holding it couldn't be ignored. He looked as comfortable standing before her in thin, soaking linen as he might look standing shirtless on the scaffolding of the building site. All the rough men of this settlement, maybe due to the dearth of women, were easy with their nudity. Yet the intimacy of seeing him in his body's linen-plastered glory struck her in a thousand competing ways. Her ears rang and her throat went bone-dry.

Clutching the blanket in her arms to get hold of herself, she forced her attention back to his bicep and the wet blob of black, spiky fur, saying, "It's just a baby porcupine."

Theo nodded. "I suspect it isn't more than a few days weaned."

Porcupine meat had been her husband's favorite meal, she remembered all too well. He would come back from hunting—during those terrible months when he was home—then toss a dead pair at her feet and demand she cook them for the evening's supper. She couldn't count how many times she'd been jabbed by the spines she'd had to pluck—and hurt in other ways when she didn't cook it fast enough or to his liking. And here Theo was, cradling the wild, spiny thing.

She shifted her gaze from the pup to the man, keeping her eyes above his chin as best she could. "You risked your life in that current for a baby porcupine?"

"I'm a strong swimmer." He grinned, his shirt finding new purchase clinging to a dark nipple, alert from the cold. "The little thing was falling off the timber."

"It isn't going to be grateful," Etienne warned. "Look. It's starting to raise its ruff."

Theo bent at the knees and set the writhing thing on the grass. The pup rolled onto his taloned paws and shook himself, white-tipped quills alert. With its tiny front paws, it began wiping moisture off its snout.

Etienne. Orphans. And now he'd saved a porcupine. Saints alive, what was she supposed to think of this man?

"It looks fine." Theo jerked his chin toward the resin-scented woods behind her, with its carpet of russet needles. "It'll wander off to safety once we get out of its way."

"Yes," she said, coming to her senses and marshaling up what courage she could. "We should get back to where we belong, too. Monsieur Martin, would you mind carrying the canoe back to its berth?"

"Mother." A black look passed over Etienne's face. "I can carry the canoe—"

"I know you can. You're strong enough. But I want..." *Theo's hands occupied, and you far away, when I ask him difficult questions.* "I want you to fetch the basket and oars and take them back. I'll carry this blanket." She ran her wretchedly shaking hand over the wool. "That way we won't have to make several trips."

Despite the practical answer, Etienne narrowed his black eyes as he looked from her to Theo and then back to what she supposed was her pale, pinched face.

"Go on ahead, now." She lifted her skirts and edged around the young porcupine, still occupied with cleaning its bristles. "I have business with Monsieur Martin, *tsítsho*."

Etienne's expression flickered. Since his childhood, they'd used that Mohawk word for fox as a signal that all was well. They had another word to indicate danger, but she'd rarely used it. If she had been in danger from his father in those days, the last thing she wanted was little Etienne to stick around to witness it.

Casting a last, sullen look at Theo, Etienne walked down the bluff, grabbed their food basket, and shouldered the oars. Theo followed a few steps behind to fetch the vessel itself, saying something jocular to her son as he passed. A query that Etienne ignored, stewing.

She should scold Etienne for rudeness, but suspicion of big, strong men was tough to shake for *both* of them. Instead, she watched Theo haul the canoe up and over his head as if the vessel were constructed of feathers. His bare thighs flexed as he climbed the steep slope, his hands on the gunwales, arms bulging. The soaked linen shirt still clung to the parts of him she had no business noticing—though she *did* notice his high, flexing buttocks as he marched by her. She followed, heart halfway up her throat, body tingling in unnerving ways, and her mind smoking from the burning effort to make sense of a confounding situation.

As she lagged behind, he said, "You've been avoiding me, Cecile. Me and the children. They've been asking why you haven't come for lessons."

Flinching, she tightened her grip on her skirts and raised the hem above her boots. "Mother Superior is due back any day now." A lame excuse— the Reverend Mother had warned Cecile that her stay in Quebec would likely be extended—but how quickly came the lie! "I haven't finished the accounts, so I couldn't spare the time to go out to the stable."

"The kids miss you."

Guilt shot a dart through her. She would make it up to them, whenever she figured out how dangerous this man was.

"Cecile." He slowed his pace so she would reach his side, shifting the weight of the vessel hanging above him. "Don't let me—and whatever you think of me—prevent you from teaching those kids."

"Frankly," she said, hurling herself into the breach, "I don't know what to think of you."

"On the contrary." His voice dropped. "You think the worst of me."

She wanted to say *Of course I do,* but it wasn't completely true. She had witnessed him being kind, generous, and charitable—to a point she couldn't ignore. But she'd also witnessed his violence.

"Your crime…" she forced words past a barrier of her own making. "Was it a bloody one?"

He paused for only a moment.

"Yes."

She stumbled over nothing as a burst of white light emptied her mind. Theo shifted the weight of the canoe to fling out a hand toward her, but she ducked it. She found her feet and struggled to get herself steady, realizing as she fell into pace that she didn't want to hear any more about the nature of his crime.

She'd heard all that she needed to know.

Girding her courage, she flung an accusation instead. "That's why you kept your incarceration a secret."

"I didn't keep it a secret." He gripped the canoe with both hands again. "The man who owns my papers should have told Mother Superior in the letter he sent her, but apparently, he didn't. Knowing the man, I'd say he didn't want to risk the outrageous wages she'd agreed to pay for my labor."

"Still," she said, bile rising at her daring, "you didn't tell *me.*"

"Because you flinch in my presence—and have done so long before you learned I'm a convict."

Heat swept up her cheeks. Of course she'd flinched the first time she'd met him. She shouldn't be ashamed, but she had struggled long and hard to contain the uncontrollable terror—had even taken pride in small successes. She couldn't let her husband win—she'd long vowed not to spend the rest of her life shrinking like a coward in the presence of the rougher sex.

And yet Theo had noticed not just the flinch, but he'd figured out *why* she flinched.

What else had he noticed about her?

Don't think about that now. "You didn't tell me about your prison sentence," she blurted, "but apparently you had no qualms telling Jules."

"I didn't tell Jules. I didn't tell anyone."

"Then how did he know?"

"People talk." The canoe he carried wobbled as he stepped over a divot in the grass. "The man who holds my contract spends a lot of time in taverns. As does Jules."

She looked down at her boots, wondering if Jules had known her husband, who'd also spent lots of time in taverns.

"Cecile," he said, in that intimate way, "has there been any trouble on the building site since I've taken over?"

"Yes. You nearly broke Jules's jaw."

"I did that to protect you." He dipped his head so he could meet her eyes from below the canoe. "You must know that."

Her heart had risen so high in her chest that it felt like it clogged her throat. She had no words, anyway. She wasn't so foolish as to ignore that he'd jumped down from the scaffold for the sole purpose of protecting her. But she didn't know how to feel about it. Or maybe she just didn't *want* to feel the gratitude, the surge of warmth…or the sense of being cocooned in safety by a man who wasn't the least bit safe.

She stayed mum and fixed her attention on Etienne's stiff back as he strode ahead of them. She noticed how the grass in this part of the field had grown wild. The fruited heads brushed against her skirts and left little seeds and burrs behind. Every step launched another grasshopper in a flying arc. Crickets sang in the weeds, and barn swallows swooped and looped in the sky above them.

Three-quarters of the way across the field, he broke the silence. "Do you have a problem with my work? Or with how the building is going up?"

"Of course not." It would have been so much easier if Theo had been a lazy worker. But Theo guided the men without arguing about their mistakes. The laborers ran to consult him about everything. He always had a trowel in his hand, spent most of his time on the scaffold, didn't toss orders for the sake of shouting, didn't swagger and boast, but kept his head down. He was a man roped with muscles, a creature capable of building and destroying in equal measure, who channeled his strength into something else, something solid and lasting. "I'm quite sure Sister Martha will be thrilled at the progress when she returns."

"Then it's just me—the man—that you're afraid of. Is that why you're wearing the gray habit of the congregation today?"

She glanced down at her stiff skirts. There were loads of reasons why she'd decided to shed her yellow dress. A woman who intended to become a nun might as well get used to the dull, coarse clothing she'd wear for the rest of her life. A woman in a habit received fewer stares and propositions when walking about the market square, visiting the Lachine Rapids, or wandering through a building site. All good reasons, but not the main one. She wore this habit to remind herself how she'd vowed to avoid the company of strong, dangerous, unsettling men altogether—whether the Reverend Mother consecrated her into the congregation or not.

"It shouldn't matter to you," she said, kicking sheafs of upright grasses, "what I wear."

"You think it'll keep men at bay." His voice tightened like the knuckles of his hands. "But a man with truly bad intentions won't let a nun's habit stop him from taking what he wants. Is that what you think I'll do?"

"I told you." Nausea rose along with a pounding in her temples. "I don't know what to think of you."

Her foot scuffed against hardened ground. They'd reached the area beyond the grassy field where the canoes were stored under a brace of pines by the convent schoolhouse. Etienne waited there, leaning against the schoolhouse wall, his fierce gaze fixed on them. Theo shot a few steps ahead of her, overturned the canoe and laid it on the hard-packed ground next to the others.

When Theo straightened, her heart did a double thump as his pale gaze of green pinned her.

"You're not going to ask anything else about my crime?"

She threw a palm up. "It's not my business—"

"You mean it doesn't *matter*." His eyes narrowed as he took a step toward her. "A dirty criminal is just a dirty criminal, right?"

The fierce, angry words hit her like a whip snap. He'd read her wrong. But she couldn't calm his affront without revealing some secrets of her own.

"Hey." Etienne strode in front of her, all puffed up. "No one talks to my mother like that."

"Etienne." She placed a hand on his shoulder.

"Mother, he's been bothering you since—"

"Enough." She whispered the word. Etienne went silent. Theo, too. "Sir." She turned her attention back to Theo and forced her voice even. "I thank you for bringing the canoe back for us. I will see you tomorrow morning for our usual discussion."

She headed toward the convent schoolhouse, nudging Etienne to come along with her, only to stop as a black ball of spines waddled across their path. The porcupine continued on its way, chaff and seeds caught amid its quills from the long trip across the field. It stopped, snuffling, by Theo's bare feet. Theo crouched down and swept it up into the crook of his arm again, where it burrowed.

By all that was holy.

Even wild things trusted this man.

CHAPTER NINE

She's coming.

In the shadowed edge of the woods, Theo sat at the foot of a maple tree, watching as Cecile left the convent schoolhouse and strode across the sunset-streaked field toward the stable, where the children waited for lessons. At the sight of her, Theo sagged against the rough bark, exhaling long and slow though he hadn't been aware of holding his breath. He couldn't fully say why he was lurking here in the forest shadows, guts bunched in knots, wondering if she would keep her promise and resume lessons.

He knew only one thing—his relief at seeing her wasn't solely for the children.

Now, digging his fingers into the leaf-litter, he drank in Cecile Tremblay in a way he would never do when she could see him. The toes of her boots jutted from under the hem of her gray novice's dress with every kicking stride. Her head bowed over that lovely neck, where her hair lay coiled so tight that he couldn't help fantasizing about yanking out the pins and watching it tumble down her back.

As she neared the stable, Theo flattened a hand on the ground and considered pushing himself up and shouting her name—no, not her name. Calling her Cecile unsettled her more than anything. Her throat would flush rosy. He suspected she would blush in other places, too, but that damn nun's habit covered her from neck to wrist to ankle and silently screamed—*Stay away, you violent brute.*

He closed his eyes as frustration tightened into a spiny lump in the pit of his stomach. Despite their talk yesterday, he knew she was still wary of him, but why did her opinion bother him so much? He'd long shielded himself from caring about such things, yet here he was, lurking, when he should be bedding down in the laborer's cabin for the night—and reminding himself that, once he was free, he had a life to resurrect and family back in France depending on him.

None of his plans allowed room for Cecile.

Six weeks and five days.

The porcupine pup, tucked into a tuft of grass at the foot of the tree, snorted in her dozing, as if she could sense Theo's unease. Twice, he'd carried the pup into these deep woods to set her free. Twice, she'd followed him back by scent and stubbornness. She wouldn't even stay in the stable with the kids, who'd tried to win the pup's favor by feeding her acorns, twigs from maple and oak trees, and the occasional slice of green apple. The critter hadn't shot a quill at anyone yet, but more than once she'd ruffed up when startled. Bringing to mind another prickly female he knew.

The faint creak of leather hinges brought his head back up, just in time to see the flash of Cecile's heels as she entered the stable. Inside, Jeanne squealed, and the boys shouted greetings. Yes, he'd done the right thing in keeping his distance, if only for the kids' sakes. He should get up and cross over to the laborer's cabin now, get some sleep, but his backside remained on the ground. Stewing over the matter longer than he should, he scratched the little spot the porcupine liked, just under her chin, before leaning back against the rough bark and closing his eyes in frustration.

When he lifted his head again, the bright sunset had given way to the gloaming. He must have dozed. Church bells clanged in the distance. At first, he thought they were vesper bells, maybe compline. But the ringing was less rhythmic and more discordant than for ordinary canonical hours. He pushed away from the tree, stepped out from under the canopy, and squinted west. Past the thick stand of pines that separated the convent grounds from the outer edge of the settlement of Montreal, a red glow bathed the sky.

From the road came a shout.

Fire!

Panic kicked him. Theo dropped into a run, bolting across the field. He knew the wooden buildings on Saint Paul Street sat cheek by jowl, which made Montreal a tinderbox. Against his cheek, he felt the gust of a northeasterly breeze, the kind that might carry sparks to the stand of pines, or even to the convent schoolhouse itself.

As he passed the stable, he saw François and Jeanne burst through the door, shouting and pointing west. A bewildered Cecile emerged last, fumbling with gathered slates.

He shouted to the children while in a full run. "Get buckets. All the empty ones you can find."

"There's some in the laundry." Cecile tossed her burden of slates aside. "I'll fetch those."

She charged across the field, the golden roll of hair bobbing, the kids following in her wake. Then, forcing all thoughts of Cecile Tremblay out of his mind, he continued his race toward the road, shouting to the laborers pouring out of the log bunkhouse to join him for the quarter-mile sprint to the settlement.

As stabbing pains dug into his lungs, he approached the outer edge of Montreal. Theo noted that the fire raged closer to the fort, on the far western end of the settlement. But as he'd suspected, the wind had carried sparks east. Those sparks had landed on the thatched roofs of several buildings, roofs that had not seen rain in weeks. Madness, it was, that after thirty years of settlement and dozens of infernos, these wooden houses hadn't been replaced with stone.

He jogged down the riverside Saint Paul Street into the eye-watering burn of falling ash. Women with babes in their arms ran in the opposite direction. Older people were being pushed in carts.

Beams cracked, and a house caved in just ahead. Embers rained down, searing his forearms and hair. He paused, assessing the situation. The house that had just cratered was lost, and the one beside it, nearer to him, was already aflame. But the merchant shop next in line was still intact save for one flickering flame on the roof.

"Here," he shouted to the milling crowd and the laborers arriving in his wake. "Form a line from the river's edge to where I stand by this shop."

Fortunately, only a narrow strip of grassy common separated the Saint Lawrence River from Saint Paul Street. The crowd fell into a rough line, some heading toward the river to fill their buckets. Within a few moments, the man beside him thrust a pail into his belly, water sloshing over the rim. Jules, Theo realized, recognizing the fire-bronzed hair, sticking up like he'd just rolled out of bed. Theo hauled up the bucket and hurled the water onto the now-growing flame on the thatch before swinging the empty back into Jules's hands.

Soon, townspeople joined the line, a crowd of merchants, servants, laborers, Abenaki who were camping in the field behind the settlement, children from the lime ricks, Etienne, convent novices, and…

Cecile.

There she was, standing between Jules and Etienne. His vision sharpened and narrowed. Her blond hair—loose in a braid that danced against her back with every exchange of buckets—might as well be a net for sparks. And her swinging skirts made for too-easy kindling. The buckets were heavy, and as she sank under the weight of one, Jules relieved her of it.

Theo opened his mouth to shout for her to leave—they had enough men on the line—but Jules's full bucket hit him in the solar plexus, turning the shout into an *oof.* Grunting, Theo swung it up and emptied the water over the thatch. When he thrust the bucket back into Jules's hands, he glared at Cecile over the ruff of Jules's red hair in an effort to catch her eye.

When he did, he willed her to read his mind.

Get out of here.

Her dark eyes flashed before she showed him her back, defiant in this as in so many things. He knew the Reverend Mother had tasked her with paperwork, but he'd seen Cecile scrubbing laundry with the novices, shouldering food sacks into the storehouse, and hauling platters of meat from the convent kitchens to the table set outside for the laborers' midday meal. But, damn it, a woman who looked as fragile as glass shouldn't be hauling full water buckets in the midst of an inferno.

Go back. Fetch more buckets, he mentally screamed.

She didn't look up at him again.

Seizing another bucket from Jules, he aimed with all his might, making the best of his frustration. Droplets of water dripped from the eaves—a sign that even his best efforts were not effective to douse the far side of the roof, which needed just as much soaking. He glanced around, spied a mason coming late to the fire, and shouted for him to return to the building site to fetch a ladder.

The sound of cracking wood came from the house next to the shop he was trying to save, and the roof collapsed with a thud. Grit fell from the sky, edged with fire. He was about to throw the latest bucket of water upon Cecile to soak her skirts and hair when a cry rang out. A figure shot out of the narrow alleyway between house and shop. Her skirts trailed fire as the screaming woman ran, tripped on a rut, and sprawled.

He shot the contents of the bucket meant for Cecile at the woman instead. Jules followed with another bucket. Cecile shot to the woman's side and doused the last of the flaming skirts. Dropping her empty pail to the ground, she fell to her knees beside the woman.

Jules pointed to the shop's roof. "New flames!"

Theo turned in time to see an ember catch, flaring up from the other side of the shop roof's peak. He stepped back into line and grabbed another full bucket just as someone planted a ladder against the shop. Seizing a rung with one hand, he climbed up until his head poked above the edge of the thatch. Heaving the bucket onto his shoulder and setting one hand flat beneath the bottom, he hurled the bucket high enough that it hit the peak and spilled its contents down the other slope.

The lick of flame dimmed. A curl of smoke rose as the bucket rolled back down toward him. Catching it, he handed it back to Jules and exchanged it for a full one, launching the contents high. He did it again with a new bucket. And then again.

"Hey!" Jules, standing on the third rung of the ladder, shouted after they'd exchanged a dozen or so more buckets. "Switch places!"

Theo thrust an empty bucket at him. "Shut up and keep the water coming."

"You want me to ignore your orders?"

What orders? "No time for this, Jules."

"We need maximum effort, right?"

Theo glowered, a look that had zero effect on this damn foolhardy mason.

"You're always going on about taking shifts so we don't get injured." Jules glanced back to exchange his empty bucket for a full one from Etienne, then bent his elbow to make his bicep swell. "So put fresh muscle into this job."

Theo frowned. "I'll switch in a minute."

"I'm holding you to that."

Jules held up the full bucket, grinning, Theo grabbed it and aimed the water over the peak again.

He supposed this was as close as Jules would ever come to apologizing for what an ass he'd been. But Theo wasn't in the mood to share a tankard of ale with him yet.

After he'd thrown a half-dozen more buckets, he glanced Cecile's way and found her standing with her hands on her hips, shouting something to the crowd. The burnt, injured woman was shaking on the ground behind her.

"Take over." He thrust an empty bucket at Jules and kicked off the ladder, landing hard on the flats of his feet. Three strides shortened the space between him and a distressed Cecile. "What do you need?"

"A blanket." Black spots marred her light gray skirts where sparks had burned the fabric. "The woman has burns and is soaked and cold."

Cold, while an inferno blasted? That didn't bode well for her recovery, nor did the angry red blisters visible under the burned holes of her still-smoking stockings.

Frowning, he seized the collar of his shirt, measured the value of his pride, and then yanked the hem free from the waistband of his sagging breeches. Hauling the shirt over his head, he thrust it at Cecile, who'd gone still.

"This will have to do," he said, "until you can fetch a blanket from the convent."

She dragged the cloth from his hands. For pride's sake, he waited until she was shifting her attention back to the woman before he turned toward the bucket line, exposing to her—and all of Montreal—the shame of his naked back.

Despite the roar of the flames, the rattle of buckets, the collapse of beams, and pounding feet, he heard Cecile's gasp.

CHAPTER TEN

Back on the convent grounds, in the dim quiet of night, Cecile yanked the cork from a wine bottle, tossed it on the riverbank, and took a long, deep pull. The sweet red wine slipped down her throat like cool satin. She sighed at the warmth spreading through her and sank back on the brace of one hand to lift her gaze to the heavens.

A smoky haze from the inferno still hung between land and sky, dimming the view of the stars and filling the air with the stink of ash. But the red glow in the west had disappeared now that the fire was quenched. Toward the east came a faint lightening, the first hint of dawn. The Saint Lawrence River lapped against the shore beyond her feet, a siren's call to strip down and wash the grit from her hair and skin.

But right now, the wine was doing valiant work calming her after the trauma of the inferno…and the searing memory of a bare-chested Theo, battling the flames like some warrior in a hero's tale.

She took another long draw of wine.

"Can't sleep?"

She didn't flinch. She hadn't heard Theo's approach but, if she were honest, she'd admit—at least to herself—that she'd *chosen* to come to this quiet, secluded riverbank in the hope that he would eventually follow.

She'd seen the scars on his back.

She had so many questions.

"Here." Head averted, she thrust the bottle at him, wondering if he was still bare-chested, taking a moment to gather her wits in case he was. "This might help with sleep, if you're struggling too."

He folded his stone-muscled body to the ground beside her before taking the bottle from her hand. So careful, he was, to not touch her fingers. How did he know that he unsettled her? His simple presence— even now—stole her breath, set her heart pounding, and made her stomach knot with uncomfortable feelings she couldn't name.

No. I mustn't be a coward. She braced herself, swiveling her head to face him—only to discover Theo had cleaned up, his hair damp and showing the tracks of a comb, his chest covered by a clean linen shirt. Another uncomfortable feeling spiraled through her, but it wasn't relief.

Take hold of yourself, Cecile.

"Those burns." She shifted her gaze to the blisters rising on his knuckles. "I have an unguent back at the—"

"No need." He took a swig of wine and wiped his lips with his sleeve. "My hands are hardened from mortar—I don't feel the sting. Save the ointment for others who need it."

Of *course* he'd say that. She turned away from the sight of his long, strong throat as he swallowed. She fixed her gaze on the far shore, where the forest stretched as black as ink, as impenetrable as the nature of this convict who'd saved her son's life and kept a baby porcupine as a pet. A man whose whip-disfigured back reminded her that he'd committed a terrible crime and bore the scars of the consequences.

Never, ever would she be able to put together the pieces of this man in a way that made sense.

Why did she keep trying?

"Such a destructive fire." An inane thing for her to say, but she needed a safe topic of conversation. "I counted at least a dozen homes destroyed."

"Several warehouses as well." He offered her the bottle. "It'll take a week for the wind to blow away the stink of burnt pelts."

"The hospital was spared, at least." She took the bottle but didn't drink. She was already dangerously light-headed. "I heard a rumor that a woman started the fire, a servant—"

"A Mohawk captive," he corrected. "Or so said the crowd shouting accusations in the street."

She heard the suspicion curdling his words. "You think they're wrong?"

"A fire could be started by anything." He pulled a piece of grass out of the ground and shredded it. "A spark rising from a chimney. A torch fallen from a sconce. A badly stacked hearth fire spilling beyond the hearthstone onto a basket of wool."

"Or arson," she added. "How else would the rumor start? Maybe someone saw the woman set the fire and reported it."

"Everyone wants a scapegoat." He tossed the fragments of grass away and brushed the remnants off his breeches with more force than necessary. "And the authorities need somebody to hang."

The question shot to her lips—*were you a scapegoat?*—but she stopped it behind her teeth. Until this past June, she had fervently believed that everyone who had been convicted of a crime was a wicked, unredeemable villain. *After* June, she'd spent every day and every restless night trying to convince herself that some crimes could be justified…because if she was mistaken about that, then *she* was an unredeemable villain.

Etienne, too.

"Theo." His name fell from lips on a breath, as did the question to which she now needed an answer. "What were you convicted of?"

"Theft," he answered, as if he'd been expecting that query from her forever. "Theft and murderous assault."

She flinched, remembering Theo grappling on the dusty ground with Jules. Dear heavens. A smarter woman would have stomped on her own curiosity and continued to avoid Theo in an excess of caution, but instead, here she was—*reckless fool*—tearing down the wall between them. She raised the bottle and took another hefty swig, then settled it on the grass.

His voice rumbled in the darkness. "You're still here."

"I am." As foolish as it might be.

"Most people would run away." His chest rose. "After all, you're sitting alone with a violent criminal on the banks of the river under the cover of night, so far away from others that no one would hear you scream."

Her throat tightened. "I know."

"You're a brave woman, Cecile. In so many ways."

She didn't feel brave. She felt confused, conflicted, and addled to the point of being unable to make sense of the storm of feelings the presence of this man set loose inside her. She couldn't look at him right now, yet she was intimately attuned to his breathing, to the warm, muscular bulk of him shifting at her side. Though every tendon in her body vibrated, she couldn't even tell if that trembling was due to fear.

"Thank you," Theo murmured into the silence. "I almost forgot what trust feels like."

Did she trust him? She knew better than to trust *any* man. A new pressure rose up in her chest, the front wave of the old terrors. To hold it off, she blurted, "Are you guilty of those crimes, Theo?"

"Not of theft." He leaned back on his hands, the muscles in his arms bulging under his weight. "But I am guilty of murderous assault."

Such a casual confession of a brutal crime, the words ringing in her ears. "So…you murdered a man?"

"No." His jaw tightened. "Though, in the moment, I wanted to, very much."

His words kicked her, but not in a way that thickened the pressure in the back of her throat, or set her stomach dropping. Instead, those words jolted through her in bright recognition, for she knew how it felt to want someone dead with every fiber of her being.

"I'll tell you the story," he continued against the shush-shush of the lapping river. "I've got nothing to hide. Every spring, we—the stonemasons of Guéret—made a pilgrimage out of our village to find work in the bigger cities. That year, I led a crew toward Paris, where we had already been hired to raise a city building."

She imagined Theo on the roads, trowel tucked into his belt, a linen bag slung across his body, men following in his wake. Easy to imagine, for she'd seen how well he worked with others upon the scaffolding and, tonight, how men during a fire followed his lead without question.

"We weren't far outside the gates of Paris," he continued, "when I noticed a stopped carriage and the coachman sitting across the road with his back to it. I thought the coach needed repair for a broken axle or something. Then, on the ground by it, I noticed an overturned basket of posies. The kind of flowers poor girls gather in the fields outside the city, around that very road, and then head to Paris to sell on the streets for a trifle."

She sensed how this story would unfold as an image of Theo hurling himself toward Etienne to save her son shot through her mind.

"The coach was shaking," he said. "Noises came from inside, a girl's muffled cry—"

"It's hardly a crime to save a girl's honor," she interrupted to stave off the grim details.

"It's a crime," he corrected, "when the man who abducted the girl from the fields is a viscount."

She bent her knees up to her chin. "He was a nobleman…and you set your fists flying, didn't you?"

He shrugged. "My men pulled me off the beast before I could do too much damage. The viscount was bloody, roaring with fury, but the masons hurried me off to Paris. No sign of the girl anywhere. She'd grabbed her basket and run away."

Cecile knew why the girl had run. There was no remedy for that kind of assault, not for the victim.

Not even if the poor girl had been the viscount's wife. Noblemen committing that kind of violence considered it their privilege, and so remained unrepentant, unpunished, undaunted. Free to commit the same crime again, over and over.

Cecile rocked, forcing back memory, aching from the depths of her being for an impossible wish—that, back before that terrible June, she had had a defender as strong and big and reckless as Theo, willing to risk his own life to pull a monster off of her, and set her and Etienne free.

"Unfortunately," Theo continued, lost in his own story, "the viscount was too full of pride to put the situation behind him. He searched for me in Paris. I wasn't hiding, we of Guéret stay in the same neighborhood every year. He chose to have me arrested. I was hauled off, kept in shackles, and didn't know until I was dragged into court what I was charged with. He claimed I'd stolen his ornamental dagger, which I had knocked out of his hand so he wouldn't disembowel me while fighting. He said I'd tried to kill him with it."

"But you had witnesses." A lump hardened in her gut, for surely the purpose of the courts was to find justice. "Your fellow masons saw what happened. They supported your side of the story?"

"They did." His voice curdled with bitterness. "But laborers from Guéret are strangers in Paris, foreigners who eat odd things and speak a different dialect. Our testimony had no impact on the judges, who knew the viscount and his family."

"But the girl…" A cold hand closed over her heart. "Certainly, she testified to—"

"They didn't bother to find her." He shook his head. "A woman's testimony isn't held in high regard in the courts, Cecile."

She winced at that truth. She knew that justice— at least the frontier justice of Montreal that she was familiar with—wasn't always full of mercy and grace. She'd seen the mutilations of men in the settlement and knew of the hangings in Quebec. But weren't there valid reasons to assault someone?

"In the end," Theo said, sitting up straighter, "the judge convicted me but offered me a choice of punishments. Four years on a galley ship in the Mediterranean or four years of indentured servitude here."

"Why did you choose to be shipped across an ocean?" She lifted the bottle of wine again, giving her hand something else to do than give in to the ridiculous urge to reach out, to touch him, to ground the vibration humming between them. "At least on a galley ship, you wouldn't be far from home."

He fixed his attention on the eastern sky, hiding his face from her sight. A moment passed and another, the hoot of an owl joining the music of the ever-murmuring river.

"When I first arrived in Montreal," he said, tilting his head back to look at the stars. "I was surprised to see the same constellations that I used to view from a mountaintop above my village." He pointed. "That's Ursa Major, that's Cygnus, and that gathering of stars that looks like a W is Cassiopeia. To see the same constellations here as in France seemed odd to me. I had come here, hoping this world would be different. I chose exile over a galley ship because I *wanted* this world to be different."

"That's why I came here, too, in a way." She remembered the naïve girl who'd left the security of an orphanage for the dangerous unknown with a head full of foolish dreams. "But the nuns are right: Everything is wild in this place—the flowers as well as the men."

"That wilderness is untouched. I hope it remains that way." He jerked his chin toward the inky, impenetrable blackness of the forest across the river. "Out there, only natural law rules. I think that's why so many Frenchmen lose themselves in the woods. From what I've seen, the law is as cruel here as it is back in France. Here, even my master can whip me to death, legally, for any reason—or for none."

"Why haven't you run away?" The woods seemed a natural choice for this strong, proud man. "They'd never find you out there, Theo."

"My conviction and my exile from home have consequences for my family. I am the oldest, and they depended on me. I have to make it all up to them, someday. I can't do that if I'm running from the law." He straightened up a fraction, shaking his shoulders as if shaking off a burden. "It's not a pretty story. But you believe me, don't you?"

"Yes." She cast him a glance, seeing the stillness of his expression and the hope banked in his eyes. "I believe every word, Theo."

He made a strange, glottal sound, then dropped his head to stare at the ground, brow rippled.

"Is it…" He stopped, took a breath. "Is it because you've known violence yourself?"

"No." Maybe *yes*, but she still couldn't admit that to him. Not yet. "It's just that I've come to know you. There's more to you than the crime they accuse you of."

Heavens alive, why had she said that out loud? She stopped rocking, caught up in a stillness she had no explanation for. She sensed his sudden intensity, though she dared to look at him only out of the side of her eye. What sort of dark magic did this huge, powerful man wield, to make her feel unafraid while alone in his presence?

"Cecile."

She watched his lips form her name. She saw the way starlight gleamed in the bristles of his unshaven cheek. No part of him touched her, yet she felt held. Not held. Cosseted. This was a man who could protect her, as he'd protected that poor girl, as he'd protected Etienne. Theo would never hurt her. With that realization reverberating through her body, an otherworldly calm came from nowhere and suffused her blood, tendons, and bones, even as Theo moved close enough for his breath to brush her cheek.

"I know I shouldn't do this." He grazed his knuckles against her jaw, turning her face toward his. "Maybe you'll forgive me later."

He brushed his lips against hers.

CHAPTER ELEVEN

A breath of a kiss. That had been Theo's intent. At the first touch of their mouths, her lips felt wet and tasted of wine. He lingered just a moment, anticipating a flinch or gasp. He waited for a sign, for then he would pull himself back before her fear bloomed. A wiser man might have chosen another way to thank her for trusting him. He was likely conflating a carnal urge to seize her with a loftier goal to prove to her that not all men were brutes. Cecile was a beauty his body hungered for, but she was also the only true gentleness he'd encountered in years.

Marshaling his will, he pulled away a fraction. Her lower lip clung to his for a moment before separating.

There.

It was done.

Their faces hovered as closely as two people could without touching. Through his lashes, he saw, even in the dim starlight, a spray of freckles across her nose and cheeks, kissed darker by sun during the summer weeks. He began to count them—a way to distract himself from wanting too much from her. As he did, the wind soughed through the pines at the edge of the woods while the river sang its gurgling song.

Cecile.

Her name rang in his head like a prayer. He yearned to whisper it aloud. In a moment—any second now—she would bend back, shuffle across the grass, or stiffen into stone. She'd turn her face away and lift her chin and raise the walls she'd built between them.

As the moment stretched, his control wavered, cracks spidering through. Why had he thought kissing her would ease her fears or increase her trust in him?

Was he mad to believe he could resist temptation? His count of her freckles passed twenty-five and still she remained unmoved, eyes lowered but lashes fluttering. He dug his fingers into the grass, wondering, for the first time, if it could possibly be affection—or desire—that held her in thrall.

Didn't matter. He should be the one to put an end to what he'd started.

The grass ran smooth under his hip as, against all desire, he slid himself away, pulling back from the promise of those parted lips, that gleaming mouth.

"No."

She whispered the word and seized him with her dark, churning gaze.

His pulse jumped. He'd watched her mouth form the word, but what did she mean? Was she finally coming to her senses and telling him that she didn't *want* to be kissed? Or did she mean... Did she want him to—

No, he shook off the idea. It was madness to let his wishful hopes rise.

He glanced down at his hand splayed against the ground to find her warm, paler one sliding over it. The wind stopped sighing in his ears and the stars tilted in his sight.

"Don't stop, Theo."

The whispered command burrowed deep. His control fell away. His palm ached to feel the brush of her hair against it—and now his hand filled with the silky warmth, gritty with ash, damp in places. He cupped her head, guiding her so he could set his lips against hers with the urgency he'd held leashed for too long. Their bodies pressed together. Ripples of sensation vibrated through him.

He could feel them rippling through her, too.

Easy, easy, whispered his better nature as he covered her mouth with his. He'd banked these urges but now there was no holding back the surge. As he tilted his head to tease her lips apart, justifications burbled and roiled—Cecile had been married, her husband was lost to the wilderness, she was no virgin feeling a man's touch for the first time, she knew what this kind of kissing led to, he could *feel* that she wanted him.

He coaxed with the tip of his tongue to open her mouth—then she moaned.

A low sound, a flutter of the larynx.

White light exploded in his mind. He curled his other arm around her. He knew he could shift her down to the grass, tug her skirts over her thighs, touch her in all the places he wanted to taste. She would arch her back in excitement when they joined together. He knew she would.

Dark thoughts gathered. He would make it good for her. He would make her scream his name. In the long years to come, she would remember their merging, hungry bodies moving as one toward joy on the banks of this river.

She would remember *him*.

The madness of that thought jolted him back to sanity. Here he was, eroding her will with a promise of pleasure when he didn't know what she wanted— or if their minds were as one. Wasn't he just a laborer in tattered breeches, a convicted felon who had nothing to offer this woman but an evening's delight?

Cecile deserved a thousand times better.

Damn it.

He yanked back far enough for the cool air to sweep between them.

"Cecile."

Her name was all he could manage.

She breathed words he could barely hear but sounded to his hopeful ears like "Don't stop."

No, she didn't mean that—she could hardly raise her head or hold his gaze.

He glanced to the ground to see the bottle of wine they shared was overturned and drained. Had she taken more than a few gulps? He hadn't been paying attention.

As the moment of their separation stretched, her breath grew less shallow, her gaze steadier.

"Oh." Her voice was breathy and low. "Oh, Theo, I'm…I'm—"

"Blame it on the wine." He nudged the bottle with his foot, then forced himself to face the river. He lifted one knee to hide the evidence of his desire. "Or blame it on the starlight. Or the fire."

He meant the fire in Montreal—the panic and exhaustion and the sense of intimacy that arose between people in any crisis—but he was also thinking about the burn still lighting up his blood.

"As for me," he confessed, "I've wanted to kiss you for a long time, Cecile. I still want to kiss you."

For a moment, as she slapped the back of her hand against her mouth, he regretted his honesty— but the regret lasted for only a moment. Tonight, she had revealed that she trusted him, despite his past. If he lied about how he felt, he would destroy that fragile trust altogether.

"Don't worry." He mustered the last of his better nature and muscled to his feet. "I won't let that happen again."

Unless you want it to.

Cecile heard the words—not from Theo, now striding away in the darkness—but only in her head.

In dizzy confusion, she remembered that her husband—before he was her husband—had once stolen a kiss, too. Her *first* kiss. It had been a starry night in the upper town of Quebec in mid-September, like now. She remembered the gritty cobblestones beneath her boots. She remembered her pulse racing as the man who had just proposed marriage after ten days of courtship seized her in the shadows. She remembered the violence of his hard mouth and the unwanted and unsettling things the kiss theft did to her body and how her senses were clouded long after they broke apart and she ran back, confused, to her bed.

She'd figured, in her innocence, that was the way between men and women. So she'd chosen to cede to her husband's authority in this matter—which led to the hell that followed.

But you know now, said a whispered voice in her head. *Theo's kiss wasn't stolen or violent.*

She swallowed hard, the pointed claws of fear threatening to scrape new furrows inside her. Groping for clarity, she let herself admit that Theo hadn't grabbed her. He had given her a choice after the first touch of their lips. She'd had more than a moment to say *no,* as better sense demanded. It had been her *choice* to be kissed. But she hadn't expected a simple kiss to so quickly stifle the memory of all those terrible years of her marriage—or allow her imprudent younger self to emerge in foolish glory. That naïve girl with the hungry heart had once yearned for the kind of gentleness that Theo offered, the kind of gentleness she wanted with an ache so fathomless that, at the memory, her feet arched within the confines of her boots.

She hauled herself to her feet, swaying, and stumbled down the bank toward the siren song of the water. She didn't bother to tug free the laces of her ash-smeared habit or even remove her boots. Wading into the shallows until she stood thigh-deep in the river, she spread her arms and fell into it, letting the chill close over her head. Holding her breath, she felt the eddying of the current pull her skirts about. As she was cast in such darkness, floating weightless, her swirling thoughts slowed until she heard nothing but the pounding of her pulse in her ears. She threw her arms out and tried to will the water to seep the heat from her trembling body, calm her heartbeat, and rock her until the tremors stopped.

Instead, the wicked current tugged at her braid, like Theo's hand had when he'd cradled her head. The cool water brushed her lips and slid down her cleavage. Behind her closed eyelids, the outline of Theo's face arose, still lit by starlight and gripped by banked passion.

She shot up, struggling to pull her feet from the suck of the river bottom. Saints alive, a kiss could cause so much tumult. She knew this already, and yet here she was again, pressing a hand against her chest as if holding up the rubble of the wall Theo's kiss had shattered. The barrier she'd erected to seal off the desperate, fanciful idea that a woman like her—an abandoned baby, a despised wife—could ever be cherished, protected, and loved.

She raised her face to the heavens and allowed herself to wonder, for the first time in forever, *Am I a fool, to still hope?*

CHAPTER TWELVE

Mother Superior returned to the congregation.

From his position atop the scaffolding, Theo saw, across the roofless gape of the unfinished chapel, the Reverend Mother's stout, white-capped figure stepping out of a canoe and striding across the grassy lawn. Standing by the trestle table set out for the midday meal, Cecile waited for the head nun, her shoulders as stiff as a ship's spar.

Theo stared—he couldn't help himself. It'd be easy to think Cecile's firm stance was only a nervous reaction to the reckoning to come, for the returning nun would want a full report on the budget and the building site. But Theo knew there was more to it.

He'd been keeping his distance since their reckless kiss, not wanting to destroy this fragile trust between them. But for a few fleeting, polite, and public interactions with her since—as he left the stable before she arrived to teach the children, or in the mornings when they discussed the workings of the building site—he'd held himself apart, kept his eyes above her throat and his hands stiff at his sides, not trusting himself.

Because all he could think about, day and night, was kissing her again.

Harder.

Longer.

Theo forced his attention back to the work at hand. He slapped a dollop of mortar on the stone he'd just set, passing the flat of the trowel across it. The creak of the ladder alerted him to Jules climbing up with a fresh bucket of mortar. The burly mason slid it onto the wooden boards, then hauled himself to his feet beside Theo.

"The wind's got a chill." Jules swiped his forehead with his stained sleeve. "Feels good, but winter's coming early."

Theo grunted in agreement, welcoming the distraction as he handed Jules a clean trowel. "With luck, we can still set stone for another few weeks."

"And after that?" Jules asked, spreading a hunk of mortar and pushing it into every crevice. "Are you sending us away until the spring? I'm not looking forward to chopping wood all winter for some *habitant*. I'd rather stay here and hew bluestone for the chapel lintels or something."

"I'll keep you and the men through early October at least." He frowned, still trying to redirect his thoughts. "We should gather more fieldstone for when the building starts up again in spring. I'll talk to the Reverend Mother about—"

"Monsieur Martin."

His words ceased. He would recognize Cecile's voice from a crowd of thousands, but the uncertainty in her voice pierced him with cold. He stilled with his trowel inches above the swiftly drying mortar.

"Hey." Jules cocked his head toward the bottom of the ladder. "Don't keep a pretty woman like that waiting."

Theo gave Jules a ferocious eye, but the mason returned the look with a wicked grin. "Every fool here is hoping for her attention. But you're the only one she'll talk to—"

"Enough."

"Monsieur!"

Her voice, louder now. Theo glanced down the scaffolding, a good twenty-five feet to the ground. There she was, in a pool of nun-gray skirts, her face bleach-white as she stood next to a squinting Mother Superior.

"Sister Martha," she called up, "would like to speak with you for a moment."

Jules snickered. "Wrong woman."

Ignoring him, Theo scraped his trowel free of mortar—scraping and scraping to give himself time to compose himself—and placed the tool on top of the last stone he'd set. He swung one foot down to a rung and then another until he could hop onto the churned-up ground. Turning, he focused on Mother Superior instead of the woman he ached to seize by the arm, drag behind a wall, and kiss not-so-softly into submission.

"Reverend Mother," he said, bowing his head. "Welcome back."

"And what a welcome!" The nun spread her arms to take in the solid walls of the rising chapel. "Sir, I'm astonished. You've accomplished in my absence more than has been done in twenty years."

He absorbed the tribute with a swelling of his chest even as he strained to see, out of the corner of his eye, how Cecile reacted. Did she take note of this praise and let him rise in her estimation? No sooner had the thought darted through his mind than he batted it away. He shouldn't want her to notice. Whatever feelings had been growing between them, he had an obligation to stop those feelings *now*.

"I'd hoped for progress," the nun continued, grasping the wooden cross hanging around her neck. "I prayed fervently for it in every church and chapel in Quebec. I've been disappointed so many times before, but you've worked a miracle, sir."

"All acclaim goes to these men," he said, throwing a hand up to the workers. "They have labored long and hard. It's them you should be thanking."

"Ah, you're hiding your light under a bushel basket." The nun raised her voice. "With my thanks, gentlemen, I shall lay out a feast for you, come Sunday."

Amid the distraction of cheers, Theo couldn't resist any longer. He slid his gaze to Cecile, who had dropped her attention to the grass while flexing her fingers over a covered tray she held tucked against her side.

He couldn't help himself. Inside, he commanded her, *Look at me.*

"Well, that's settled," the nun said. "Attend me in my office later, sir. I have many questions. Come now, my dear." The nun patted Cecile's shoulder. "We have accounts to go over, and it's best to get the unpleasantness done first."

"I'll join you in a moment." Cecile jiggled the tray digging into her hip. "Monsieur Martin has not yet had his dinner. I was just setting something out for him."

The nun frowned. "You really mustn't skip a meal, sir, with all the hard work you do." The Reverend Mother slid a curious glance between them both before turning toward the main building. "Cecile, see me after."

"Yes, Sister Martha."

"You must be famished," she said gently, raising those fathomless brown eyes as the nun walked away. "You skipped breakfast."

"I started work early. I had a section to finish." It was as good an excuse as the true one—that he'd missed breakfast to keep away from the woman who was serving it.

"The food is getting cold." Cecile granted him a soft smile that was nearly his undoing. "Follow me to the table—"

"I'm not hungry."

His stomach growled.

Above, Jules snickered.

Hungry or not, Theo figured the best place for him right now was twenty-five feet off the ground.

She leaned in, whispering, "Don't be stubborn, Theo."

"Just leave it on the trestle table." It was taking all his control not to seize that pretty chin and set his lips on hers. "I'll eat it later."

"If I leave it there unattended," she argued, "your prickly pet will devour it, and you know it."

He glanced toward the table and the creature sniffing the ground beneath in search of scraps.

"Also," she said, still whispering, "because Sister Martha has returned, you and I have important matters to discuss before I go to her office to report."

She turned on a heel, heading toward the trestle table, assuming he would follow. After casting one last glare up at the grinning Jules, Theo fell in line. He kept his head down to avoid watching her walk, but he couldn't block out the swish-swish of her skirts. The night he'd kissed her—and left her on the riverbank—he'd paused in the shadows to make sure she was safe. He'd watched as she'd submerged herself in the water and then climbed out soaked, hair half undone and clinging to her neck and shoulders, looking like some unworldly river nymph pulsing with enchantment, a thing of beauty brighter than starlight.

The rattling of a tray dropped on the trestle table brought him back to that river nymph, now yanking the cloth off the food before stepping out of his way. He swung a leg over the bench and sat. The porcupine settled at his feet, wriggling snout raised in expectation.

"I'll be speaking with Sister Martha in a few moments." Cecile, standing just beside and slightly behind him, knotted her hands at her waist. "She's waiting to hear about every detail that concerns the building of the chapel."

"Leave that to me."

"In the matter of the construction, I will." She took an audible breath. "But on another matter. Well, I have made a decision."

A decision? Was this about her joining the religious congregation? Or did it have something to do with their kiss? Certainly, Cecile would know better than to confess their kiss to the nun—nothing good could come of that but having both of them expelled from the grounds—but he was at sea as to what matter bigger than that she was so concerned with.

"I've been considering this for days," she continued. "And I've decided that I'm *not* going to tell Sister Martha about your troubles with the law."

He held his spoon suspended, gravy dripping. That? He'd nearly forgotten about it. To think a single brush of his lips against hers had eclipsed the memory of his confession.

"You've been badly treated," she continued, "and I see no reason to extend the injustice."

"You have a kind heart." He glanced over his shoulder and drank in the quiver of her lower lip and the compassion in her eyes. "But, Cecile, you mustn't lie to the Reverend Mother. Tell her everything."

She reared back. "What?"

"If she finds out about my conviction in any other way but from you, she won't trust you anymore."

"But…but if I tell her, then she may send you back to the man who holds your papers—"

"Maybe."

Maybe that's for the best. Then, at least, they'd be parted. He'd be far away from the temptation to kiss her again.

"I suppose, even if I told Sister Martha about your past, she may keep you here anyway." Cecile strode around the far end of the trestle table, where she paced a short furrow. "After all, she just said you performed a miracle, and you have proven trustworthy these past weeks—"

"Except when I'm alone with you." The words rose up with a force he couldn't stop. "Except," he added, managing a rueful smile, "when I kiss you."

"Theo." Her throat flexed as she swiveled hard and laid a hand on her brow. "Let's not discuss that right now."

"Tell the Reverend Mother about my crime. You'll stay in her good graces. But keep the kiss to yourself, or she'll never take you in as a nun."

That's what you say you want, isn't it?

To never know another kiss?

Cecile took a deep breath, walking around the end of the table to come to a stop just across from him. She stood as if she had been shoved upright into one of those iron cages he'd once seen hanging from a spike high on the wall of the Paris prison courtyard. The torture cage had been fixed with spikes so that a person couldn't slump or wiggle without being pierced with dirty iron.

"Since you brought it up," she said in a low voice, "that kiss was…was lovely."

"Cecile." Cool air hit the bottom of his lungs as he sucked in a sharp breath. "That kiss—hell, I sure can't forget it."

"Theo, leave me some dignity, please."

How she flushes like the sunrise.

"It was lovely," she continued, breathless, "but I'm ashamed at my behavior."

"Your behavior?" Beneath the table, the porcupine made a mewling sound. "Cecile, you shouldn't be ashamed of what we shared—"

"Please stop."

She burrowed into herself like a frightened turtle before stretching her head high again. He despised with a new fierceness the husband who'd hurt her and made her feel *ashamed*.

"You are a beautiful, warmhearted woman." *Look at me.* "I took advantage of the moment. I can't say I regret it."

"There's nothing to regret." She grasped her own arms, digging her fingers into her sleeves. "I was a willing partner. You were kind and…restrained."

Barely, he thought.

"You also proved something to me that night. Now I know not all men are monsters."

She held his gaze, her brown eyes soft and vulnerable.

Theo had thought the Reverend Mother's earlier praise had been gratifying—restoring a measure of his self-respect—but Cecile's gentle confession propelled him a thousand miles into air so thin he stopped breathing.

"I'm grateful for the lesson," she continued, flexing her fingers on her arms, "as well as the advice about not telling Sister Martha about the kiss. Because as much as you think I'll never be a nun, I have no choice but to persuade Sister Martha to make me one."

Why?

Why be a nun when I can make you mine?

The words slammed against the back of his throat, only to shatter against the solid wall of another vow. Back in Guéret waited unfinished business, as well as a grieving mother and six sisters and two brothers too young to be burdened with family responsibilities. He'd spent four years vowing to put the pieces back together.

A future with Cecile was impossible

"I'll be working on the chapel for a few more weeks," he said, "until the temperature drops closer to freezing. I'll do my best to be a gentleman."

She ducked her head to hide a smile. "But you'll be back again in the spring to finish the chapel, Theo. Keeping your distance will be difficult."

Woman, you have no idea how difficult this is.

Even the wind conspired against them. He couldn't drag his eyes away as the breeze toyed with a few curled strands that had fallen from the pinned bun at the nape of her neck. Best to tell her his plans and leave no shred of hope between them.

"I won't be back in the spring." He dropped his voice and rose to his feet. "In five weeks and four days, I'll be a free man—sailing on a ship back to France."

CHAPTER THIRTEEN

Standing in the convent's chilly, low-ceilinged office, Cecile confessed everything to Sister Martha in one long, babbling speech.

Everything but the kiss.

"My dear girl." Mother Superior straightened amid a pile of crates. "I've known from the first that Monsieur Martin is a convict. You mustn't worry yourself about that. What's more vexing is the news that he's planning to leave the settlements and won't be back in spring."

Cecile clasped her hands before her, swallowing down a storm of feelings far stronger than vexation. She wondered: Had Theo always planned to take a ship back to France? Even before he'd kissed her senseless on the banks of the Saint Lawrence River? Or had he been just as swept away by feeling as she?

"I'm so desperately in need of masons, I can't afford to lose a one, never mind such a brilliant overseer." The nun stepped back from a shelf where she'd just placed a foot-tall statue of Mother Mary, flecked with the straw it had been packed in. "How determined is he to follow that plan, do you think? Might he be persuaded to stay?"

The thought of Theo leaving gutted her hollow. "I believe he's committed, Sister Martha. He's counting down the weeks to his freedom."

"So disappointing." The nun glanced at a teetering pile of folded parchment she'd dislodged from a satchel earlier and onto the desk. "At the post in Quebec, I picked up a letter for him among the others I gathered for Montreal. It's from a little place called Guéret—I remember he said something about coming from there. Perhaps his parents are expecting him to return home."

Cecile forced her eyes open and her chin up, forcibly crushing all her reckless flights of fancy as she changed the subject. "Mother, how do you know that he is a convict?"

"Goodness, I suspected from the first." Mother Superior plucked a piece of straw off Mary's halo. "A master mason is a skilled artisan. Such a man as our Monsieur Martin would have no reason to leave his home for this frontier—and certainly no reason to sign indentured-servant papers. Indentured servitude is for those too poor, or unskilled, to afford the journey. More likely, his servitude had been thrust upon him for some transgression."

The nun's logic was impeccable.

"Cecile, my dear girl, I hope the overseer's criminal past doesn't distress you too much." The nun tilted her head, sympathy softening her blue eyes. "We are all sinners, every one of us. By faith, I trusted Monsieur Martin to build that chapel while I was away. Just as, by faith, I trusted a curiously desperate laywoman to straighten out the accounts of our congregation in my absence." The nun ducked her head, straining her head forward. "We all deserve a second chance, do we not?"

"Of course." Cecile unknotted her hands, pushing all distressing thoughts of Theo out of her mind for now. She dropped her gaze to the papers and account books she'd put in neat piles on the nun's desk. "Though you may not feel as strongly about second chances, Sister Martha, when you hear what I've discovered about the Montreal butcher."

The nun frowned. "He's overcharging me, is he?"

"By nearly double."

"Shame on him." The nun huffed a sigh. "When I go to Montreal to deliver the post, I'll express my disappointment in the strongest terms."

"Shall we go through the accounts now?" Cecile took a step closer to the desk and trailed a finger across the book's cowhide cover. "I'm afraid they were a bit of a mess."

Sister Martha glared at the book if it were a fly in her soup. "Very well, I suppose we must."

Cecile came around to look over her shoulder as the nun sank onto the ladder-back chair with a sigh. Pulling the first paper off a pile, a summary of income and expenditures for the last few years, Cecile was keenly aware that her work would now be judged, but she was eager to lose herself and all these conflicted feelings in a blizzard of numbers.

Shaking off the sink of her spirits, she began her presentation, focusing on the overall financial health of the congregation. Talking numbers and calculations slowed her spinning thoughts, at least for the moment. This congregation was barely breaking even, but there were several areas of expense that could be reduced to put the finances in better shape. In the end she read from a list of recommendations until the nun's sigh drew her attention.

"This is all very dull, Sister Martha, I know."

"Dull, yes, but important." The nun patted Cecile's hand. "You have an ease with numbers that I cannot even aspire to. I had despaired of these accounts altogether, yet you have corrected them cleanly in your elegant script. In only a few weeks."

Then will you let me take the veil?

The question shot across her mind yet it halted behind her tongue. Standing in this room decorated with niche statues of teary icons and painted portraits of saints, she swayed with dangerous indecision. She'd never really wanted to join a convent. What she'd really wanted was *sanctuary,* safety from the law. But months and months had already passed without a whisper of danger—and now Theo had *kissed* her. Insidious thoughts slid into her mind, making her question whether such a drastic measure as becoming a nun was truly necessary.

But it was—because Theo was returning to France.

Leaving her behind.

"Sister Martha," Cecile said, gathering her breath to push the words out, "I'm glad you're pleased with my work. I'd be happy to take on the task fully…as a member of the congregation."

"Ah, yes, about that matter." Sister Martha nudged away from the desk. "While in the capital, I spoke to Intendant Talon on your behalf."

"Talon?"

Cecile grew chilled, trying *not* to think of why the nun would speak about her to the most powerful man in the government.

"Talon is the king's representative." The nun tilted her head quizzically. "Surely you know that he's in charge of you and all the King's Girls, so I stole a moment to bring up your current troubles concerning your absent husband."

Cecile flattened a palm on the desk to cover for her weakening knees. She knew Intendant Talon, with his luxurious wig of bronze curls. He had been at her Quebec wedding, a multi-couple affair that had lasted only as long as absolutely necessary for the sacrament.

After, the couples had been given glasses of brandy. Talon had raised a toast, exhorting them all to go forth and multiply. New France, he'd said, needed large and fertile families.

Cecile swallowed a prickly lump of panic. "The trouble with my husband is an ecclesiastical issue, isn't it? I thought you were planning to speak to the bishop about an annulment."

"Oh, I'll speak to him eventually—the bishop doesn't like me much right now. He thinks I'm pushy." The nun wrinkled her nose. "But, also, there can't be a discussion of an annulment unless your husband's death is confirmed. You are still bound by the old vows. You can be only a laywoman here until some greater proof comes to light."

Cecile felt like a door to an ancient keep splintering under the heave-ho of a battering ram. It seemed Mother Superior did *not* have independent power to invite her into the convent—and now the most powerful man in the settlements had been alerted to Cecile's troubles.

How long before Talon unearthed her lies?

"You've gone white as a boiled sheet." The nun bolted up from her desk to place a cool hand across Cecile's forehead. "I assure you, this is the correct path forward. Talon will start an investigation to search for your husband. Once Talon determines that you are a widow, there's no need for you to join our convent. Talon will see you married again."

"No."

The word lurched out of her. Of course, Talon would want to see her remarried to whatever bachelor would have her—but *no*. Theo's kiss had changed her. Hope had changed her. There was only one man she'd be willing to marry—and he was leaving the settlements forever.

In five weeks and four days.

"I refuse, Sister Martha," Cecile blurted, rounding the desk to head for the door. "Whatever Talon finds, I will never again marry a stranger."

CHAPTER FOURTEEN

Even with Sunday Mass bells clanging, the boisterous Moose Tavern of Montreal thrummed with shouting and song.

Theo ducked his head under the lintel and entered a crowded room full of long wooden tables, benches, and fur traders who'd just returned from the wilderness. The clatter of rolled dice mixed with the lively rhythm of rowing songs and the crackle of two blazing fireplaces meant to push back the autumn chill.

He nodded to acquaintances as he passed a card game and dodged the sultry look of a woman coming down the attic stairs. The soles of his boots stuck to the sticky slates as he glimpsed a cold, empty corner near a narrow window. Ordering a tankard with a raise of his hand, he waited until the wine arrived before settling the pewter cup on the window ledge.

Shoving a hand into his beaver-skin coat, he pulled out the letter the Reverend Mother had handed him two weeks ago.

He eyed again what he'd memorized on the outside folds. A half-torn corner bore a sketch of a man in a smock carrying a trowel, a mason's sign. Oil spots and streaks of dirt soiled the simple address: *Theo Martin, Montreal, New France.*

It had been written by his younger brother Benoit, Theo deduced from the sketch, the shaky letters, and random leanings of letters. Not by a priest transcribing his mother's own words. Certainly not by his stepfather, who'd never bothered with the stepson he'd once called a magpie in a wren's nest, stealing food from his own children's mouths.

The parchment, folded and cracked and worn to thinness, weighed nothing but pressed like a capstone upon his chest. It had been two and a half years since he'd last received any news. In earlier letters, his mother had written of one sister widowed and another running amok, of the roof thatch caving in the corner, of Benoit abandoning his lessons, the minor and unending troubles of a large family.

In the last letter, she'd confessed of a blight on the fields, a flux taking the chickens, and the shame of Theo's stepfather coming back with empty pockets from Paris again. That part, Theo knew in his bones, was *his* fault. His conviction had smeared the repute of all the Guéret masons.

Now, another letter in hand, he took a long, deep swig of wine to fortify himself for what was to come. After such a long gap since the last communication, he was sure there'd be no good news inside. But with only three weeks and five days separating him from freedom, he could at least foresee a moment when he would be able to make plans to take care of those he'd left behind.

Amid the tumult of the tavern, he cracked the wax seal, unfolded the parchment, and read.

My dear brother Theo,

I hope this letter finds you in good health. I'm currently with our band of masons building a little chateau near the king's palace in Versailles, a home for some royal dignitary who wears so much powder on his wig that the whole corps of workers double over in fits of coughing whenever he visits.

Our new master mason is Pierre Moreau, do you remember him? He took over after Dad decided he was too old for this, which happened a good eighteen months after you were sent away. Did Mother write to you about that? Anyway, Pierre tells us that our dignitary pays on time, and that's a rare thing.

So, whenever the man comes around, all powdered up, we all cough into our sleeves, try not to laugh, and later wash our throats clear with good wine at a tavern nearby.

Theo stopped reading, blinking as if the paper glowed with light. Theo's mischievous, skinned-kneed brother had been thirteen—or was it fourteen?—when Theo had last seen him, and now this boy was telling stories and bragging about drinking with his compatriots at a tavern.

I hope this letter finds its way to you, but Versailles is a tiny town, and I have little faith in a postmaster that no one in the chateau uses, preferring their private couriers. But I either write this now, or you'll have to wait another six months until I'm back in Guéret. I'll do my best to fill you in, though I don't know what Mother wrote in her last letter.

Let's see. Our little sister Leonora married this April past, not long after Easter, and her new husband, Jacques Anouilh, joined us on our trek to Versailles. Lisette is with child again. The good news is that, though Paris still snubs us, our band of masons have found steady work in Lyon two years in a row and now Versailles. Pierre is already talking about trying our luck

*next spring in Paris again, hoping for memories
to fade.*

*Jean-Luc probably won't go, though. His leg
never healed quite right after his fall off the
scaffolding last year. But that's a blessing in
disguise, because he's taken over the farming and
he's good at it. He even has the back slope
planted. How long has that been fallow? Also,
he looks after ~~our my~~ father when we're all
away.*

*Father has gone soft since you left, Theo. You
wouldn't recognize him. He hardly ever yells
anymore.*

Theo grunted, thinking, *He doesn't yell at* you,
Benoit.

His ribs squeezed but he pushed down the old
resentment. The letter carried on for a paragraph or
two about the marshy ground around the area of
Versailles, and the stench of the place, and the details
of the job. A sucking sensation drew Theo right back
to the old camaraderie, reminding him of all he'd lost
and all he'd fix as soon as he was free.

*Now I've used up nearly this whole parchment
telling you things that you probably don't care
about, considering where you are, suffering a
long sentence for a crime that didn't deserve*

punishment. I hope it gives you ease to know that, with every passing year, more architects take us on.

I think of you often, Theo. So do our sisters. We all hope you find, as your sentence comes to an end, some of the opportunity we've heard spoken of by those who set out for the colonies.

Do you remember Xavier Petit? He was terrible at mixing mortar. But he set off for the colonies last year, and his mother just received a packet of furs. He says in his letter that beaver furs are the currency in Kebec. Is that true? They certainly brought some money here. On selling them to a hatmaker, his mother earned 56 livres—almost twice what would have been his mason's pay as an apprentice.

Speaking of mothers. I've left this news for last because I know you won't be able to read more after I tell you.

Our dear, sweet mother died on the Feast of Saint Nicholas last from a complaint of the lungs.

The ground fell out from under him. He slung an elbow on the sill to keep himself upright.

She was always coughing, remember? It just kept getting worse and worse. We laid her down in the plot up on the mountain, and everyone in the village came. Lisette looks after the plot all the year round. In spring it's bursting with flowers.

In his mind bloomed a green field filled with bright blue gentians, his mother's favorite color. He used to pick them and present her with bouquets she would slip into a wooden cup and put in the center of the table, leaving them there long after they wilted.

The rest of the letter blurred.

Though our mother is gone, and Father is aging, I don't want you to think we're struggling or hungry. Our sisters are all married, and I'm a master now, making enough to keep the family as well as put away a bit for a marriage of my own someday. While I'm away with the Guéret masons, the house is being taken care of by Jean-Luc. He's also watching after Father, who keeps the garden. So, see to yourself, Theo, and don't spend a moment worrying about us.

Your beloved brother by a lot more than half,

Benoit

Just as the Mass bells of the Montreal chapel came to a ringing stop, Cecile stepped out of the birchbark canoe onto the grassy common that led up to merchant's stands. She would have preferred to stay in the convent schoolhouse today, rather than venture into this babbling crowd. This morning, however, a conversation with Sister Anne had unearthed a surprising—and stronger—argument to buttress Cecile's plea to become a nun. She couldn't wait to present that argument to Sister Martha, so Cecile had tagged along with Etienne, who paddled an extra canoe to Montreal to hold the supplies Sister Martha was gathering on market day.

Cecile was all too aware that this might be her last chance to plead with the nun before Talon's investigation unearthed dangerous secrets.

"Ceci!"

Glancing up the slope, Cecile felt her heart leap with surprise. Her old friend Marie raced toward her. The swiftness of Marie's pace made her fur-lined cloak fly open to show her protruding belly. Beyond her came Marie's giant of a husband, Captain Girard, struggling to keep his dignity while also straining to catch up to his wife.

Cecile hurried toward her friend. "Marie—slow down!"

"Sister Martha didn't tell me you were coming today." Marie flung her arms wide. "I'm so glad to see you!"

"Goodness." Cecile made an *oof* as Marie threw herself at her "Look at you, racing like that. Do you want to birth this child on the market square?"

"You sound like Lucas." Marie pressed away, eyes crinkling as the captain came up behind her. "But I've got almost a month more to go."

Cecile couldn't get over how big Marie's belly was, pressing hard against her own midriff. When she'd left the Girards' homestead earlier in the year to come to the convent, Marie's belly had been a gentle bump. "You should be sitting with your feet up in confinement."

"Would you have me tied up in a locked room? You know I couldn't bear that." Marie looked her over from head to toe. "And why on earth are you wearing that *awful* habit? Gray is not your best color—and you are no nun."

"Not yet." The matter of her joining a convent had always been a bone of contention between her and Marie, so she swiftly deflected. "You look wonderful in your autumn furs, Marie." Indeed, her friend looked so happy and bright and full of life that Cecile's heart beat sore. "How I've missed you!"

"Let's never be parted so long anymore. Wait." Marie's gaze shifted "Etienne, is that really *you?*"

Cecile glanced over her shoulder at her grinning son, who'd yanked the birchbark canoe higher on the bank.

"Madame Girard." He stepped toward them, bobbing his head at Marie. His face lit up as he glimpsed who followed. "Captain!"

"You look strong, son." The captain laughed. "From the stonework? Mother Superior told me you'd become an apprentice."

Her son beamed at his idol, and Cecile couldn't help but mentally compare the glow on his face to the dark, suspicious scowl he reserved exclusively for Theo.

"He's practically got a beard." Marie reached forward to pinch Etienne's chin. "When did that happen?"

"Too fast." Cecile nudged her son, now flushed and ducking his head. "Sister Martha is waiting for you at the dry-goods warehouse, Etienne. Go on ahead and fetch the supplies."

"I'll help with the loading." The captain slapped a hand on the boy's shoulder. "I saw the mountain of boxes and barrels Sister Martha purchased. You're going to need another set of hands."

"The men are gone. Now we can really talk," Marie whispered as they made their way up the slope. "Though I warn you, Ceci. I'm determined that the only way you and I will ever have enough time to catch up is if you agree to live with me over the winter."

"Can we not do this today?" Cecile eyed her. "You, of all people, know my plans."

"Joining the convent was always a terrible plan," she retorted, "doomed to fail. Besides, Ceci, I *need* you this winter." Marie slid a palm over the roundness of her belly. "You don't want me to be trapped in a cabin for months with a growling, sleepless father and two children in diapers to care for—"

"Stop. I've lived with you. I know that Lucas does half the work."

"You're just being stubborn." Marie pouted, though with teasing in her eyes. "Think about Etienne. He would love to spend more time in the woods hunting with Lucas."

"Yes," she conceded, "he would." In fact, after her difficult conversation with Sister Martha about Talon's investigation, Cecile *had* considered spending the winter with the Girards. Marie's isolated landholding would offer protection from the law, at least through the isolation of winter. But it would never be a *permanent* sanctuary. And, though it shamed her to admit it, living with the Girards meant witnessing, day after day, the joy and love between Marie and Lucas.

The kind of love she'd glimpsed in a kiss by the riverbank but was never destined to be.

"Oh, Ceci, I do hope you decide to stay with us." Marie bounced in her step in a way that belied the ripeness of her pregnancy. "I have so very much news to tell you! Including some about our little outlaw, Genny."

"Is Genny all right?" The only thing Cecile knew about their redheaded friend from the orphanage was that she now lived, safe from the law, in the deep wilderness with the fur trader she'd married. "She's not sick, is she?"

"She's fine—and happy. But she sent me a message through a Chippewa trader from their far west trading post. She and her husband André will be sneaking back into Montreal soon to stock up on trading goods…"

With Marie's arm under her own, walking shoulder-to shoulder, Cecile listened to her news as they merged into the crowd roaming the grassy verge of the market. Around them, several dozen canvas-covered stands stood on the grass. Cecile glimpsed Algonquin and Huron families setting up blankets piled high with beaver, martin, and fox furs. She startled as she glimpsed the blue woolen uniforms of some fort soldiers who were milling about. She swiftly tugged Marie down the road away from the kind of men who might arrest her someday.

Then she stumbled to a stop.

Marie frowned. "Are you all right?"

No, she wasn't all right, but all she could do was shake her head. For coming out of a tavern—a dozen paces away—was another person she hadn't expected to see today, striding right toward them with his head down.

"Oh my," Marie muttered, following the path of Cecile's stare. "Who's *that?*"

"Theo Martin."

She whispered his name with a quiver. Theo wore his Sunday best, his brushed-to-a-shine beaver coat flung open in defiance of the cold, the corner of a letter poking out of a pocket. In finer clothing than his mason's smock, he looked like a free man of the world, though preoccupied with some important matter. Her heart performed a tumbling twist as he came closer.

"Such a strong, dangerous-looking fellow." Marie bent her lips close to her ear. "I always figured such a man was *my* weakness, not yours."

"Stop, Marie."

She'd spoken too loudly.

Theo jerked up his head. His gait hitched as his pale green gaze—as bright as a lighthouse lantern— slammed into hers.

He blurted, "Cecile."

"Hello, Theo."

Beside her, Marie sucked in a gasp.

Cecile dipped in a bobbing little curtsey, wincing even as she did it, for Marie knew that was a nervous tic of hers. She struggled to find something to say to Theo, who looked as stunned as she felt. Every time she encountered him, she felt like she had a thousand things to say, but no capacity to speak a single word. For what was there to say, when, in three weeks and five days, their lives would head in opposite directions?

Marie broke the spell. "Sir, are you Monsieur Theo Martin?"

Theo shifted his attention to her and nodded.

"Ah!" Marie cocked her head, curiosity in her eyes. "Mother Superior just told me all about you. You are the new overseer at the chapel building site?"

Theo nodded again, this time with a bow, then his gaze returned to Cecile as if it had been stretched too long in the wrong direction.

"Sister Martha praised you to the stars." A ribbon of delight lifted Marie's voice. "Indeed, my husband, who has been wanting to build a church on our land, was so impressed he began to consider stone—"

"Cecile, there you are!" Sister Martha came up from behind them, sailing to a stop. "Etienne just told me you'd arrived. I hadn't meant to summon you to Montreal, my dear. I know how uncomfortable you are in crowds. Has there been a misunderstanding?"

"No—no." She drew in a breath, doubly rattled. "I thought—"

"You've caught us, Sister Martha." Marie pulled Cecile close to her side. "I lured her here for a long gossip. It has been forever since I've seen her. I couldn't help sweeping her away. Am I keeping her from important work?"

"Of course not, Madame Girard." The nun's blue gaze shifted among their little crowd. "But now that she's here, I could use her help. Cecile, I have a few last purchases to make, and you haggle better than I do."

"If you would excuse me, ladies." Theo broke into the conversation with a bend of his neck. "I have business in town that needs attending."

Then he was gone, leaving Cecile mentally gasping.

Marie piped up again, and Sister Martha responded, but Cecile didn't hear a word of their lively conversation. One single glance from those green, green eyes, and her yearning for his kiss roared back.

Her heart was lost.

Truly, desperately lost.

"Ah, my husband is coming." Marie, with a twist, threw an arm around Cecile's neck, whispering into her ear, "I saw lightning arcing between you two," before pulling away with a look of utter delight. "Goodbye for now, and remember my invitation. We would love to have you for the winter. We have so much to talk about!"

The captain swept Marie to his side, and Cecile was left alone with Sister Martha, the very person she'd come here to see. Yet now, somehow, the meeting with Theo had wiped away every word she'd intended to say.

"Come," Sister Martha said, gentleness in her voice. "Help me pick a copper kettle."

Cecile stumbled after her while the colors of the world twisted in her sight and wondered how on *earth* she was going to manage this situation in the brain-battered state she was in.

"There seems to be a good selection here." Sister Martha stopped at a merchant's table filled with gleaming pots and iron nails and other metallurgy. "Now that we're out of earshot of any acquaintances, tell me what is troubling your mind, Cecile."

Theo.

"T-troubling me?"

"My dear girl, you look as if a stone has just fallen on your head."

She felt that way, too. Stunned and unsteady and aching. Would every encounter with Theo over the next three weeks and two days leave her so fragile and reeling? Regret surged up her throat and twisted around in dying hope. She remembered that Theo had had a letter from his hometown poking out of his pocket. Perhaps he had been preoccupied with his coming freedom, and his journey back to France.

"Tell me the truth, Sister Martha." This wasn't what she'd planned to say but the words rose fast to her lips. "You're never going to make me a nun, are you?"

"'Never' is a harsh word, my dear." The nun's brow rippled as she examined a gleaming copper kettle. "Surely you know that I would welcome a sister as talented as you into our congregation. But only after all the complicating matters are settled.

Talon's investigators are already here, I'm told. Have you heard something? Is that why you're so addled?"

"No." She shuddered from scalp to toes. "I've heard nothing."

"Nor have I." Sister Martha spun the kettle around to check the seams. "But Talon is unlikely to say anything to me until the investigation is complete."

"Perhaps we don't have to wait that long—to make me a nun, that is." Her prepared arguments returned with new urgency. "After all, you could say that I'm already a pre…a pre…" She struggled to remember the word Sister Anne had used. "A pre…novitiate. Because I've been living at the convent, and learning about the order. If the community, all the other nuns, and yourself deem me acceptable—"

"But I don't believe you are, my dear." The nun set the kettle down with a gentle clank and turned to face Cecile. "Because there is a larger issue beyond the question of your widowhood. An issue that we have yet to discuss."

Cecile's stomach sank. She couldn't fathom what the nun was referring to.

"I have been waiting these last weeks to see if you would bring up this matter yourself." The nun tilted her head. "But in all your efforts to convince me to take you in—not once did you ever admit to a calling."

Cecile slipped a hand to her throat, as if to grasp the painted wooden cross that had once lain there, before one of her husband's creditors had ripped it from her neck for the peridot pasted at its center.

It wasn't that she hadn't considered the issue of a calling. When Etienne had paddled her to the congregation months ago, she'd spent some time in the canoe fabricating a story about having nightly visions of the Virgin Mary. But, despite her crimes and piling-up lies, she hadn't been able to lie so viciously. As a wailing child during her first year at the orphanage, she'd fallen asleep too many times on the plump, incense-fragrant lap of a softly singing novice. To lie to one about a godly calling bordered on blasphemy.

One sin too many.

Sister Martha nodded, as if she saw the answer on Cecile's face. "I make no judgment." She placed a cool, smooth hand on Cecile's knotted ones. "Few women are called by our Blessed Lord to the religious life, but a calling is a vital requirement to living among us. In all our discussions, you haven't mentioned Him at all."

Cecile opened her mouth, but no explanation came out, no defiance, nothing but a loosening of breath.

"Let me guess why you came to my convent," the nun said more gently. "You need a place to hide from the world."

Cecile's stomach flipped.

"You're not the first to come to me for that kind of protection, you know." The nun sighed. "It's a common misconception that a convent is a place to shut women away. But even in cloistered convents, the nuns are not really hiding. The world comes to *us*—to be healed, or taught, or prayed for. And in *this* congregation, I'm determined that we are not to be cloistered at all, but sent out into the wilderness to ease whatever poverty and suffering we come upon."

"That's why I chose your congregation," Cecile admitted, "so I could live safely on consecrated ground and yet have a chance to see Etienne in a monastery nearby."

"You are a loving mother. But those are *worldly* concerns. Not spiritual ones. So, even if Talon's investigation proves you a widow, I cannot take you in as a nun, my dear."

Cecile reeled back a fraction. So, Mother Superior had known from the beginning that she was an unlikely candidate. She'd fooled herself into thinking sanctuary was possible, but Marie had been right. This plan had been doomed from the beginning

That left Cecile with only one choice.

"Sister Martha, I have a request."

"Speak, child." The nun gripped the cross hanging from her neck. "You know I will do the best I can for you."

"Marie has invited me to spend the winter with her family, to help when the baby comes." Cecile braced herself. "Since you no longer need me, I'd like to leave the convent tomorrow."

CHAPTER FIFTEEN

"Theo?"

Theo, bent over a half-laden canoe in the rosy light of dawn, startled at the sound of his name spoken in a timbre that his whole body recognized. He tossed a sack into the belly of the vessel and turned. There Cecile stood, at the grassy edge of the berm, swathed in a fur-lined cloak, staring at him with troubled eyes.

The thought struck him again, the same one that had hammered him yesterday when he'd come upon her in Montreal. A man could lose himself in that swirling brown gaze for a lifetime.

"Theo," she repeated, clutching a satchel more tightly in her arms, "are you going somewhere?"

He straightened to say what must be said. "I'm leaving today."

He'd meant to tell her last night. He'd mentally written a goodbye speech. He'd even waited at the stable, intending to speak to her before she gave the kids their reading lessons. But the sight of her coming across the field with the sunset bright in her hair had knocked the breath from him. He wouldn't be able to control himself if they were alone in the darkness. He would seize her by the arms and haul her against him, talk her out of becoming a nun, and beg her to go with him back to France despite her best interests and his better sense.

"I know work is done for the season on the chapel"—her brows twitched—"but I thought you still had three weeks and a day left on your sentence."

So, she was counting, too. His ribs squeezed. "First, I'm heading downstream on the Reverend Mother's orders." He forced his voice to sound neutral. "She's sending me to talk to a landowner about building a church. After that, I'll head straight to Quebec."

She nodded, ducked her head, and tightened her grip on her satchel. He stared at the part in her hair, the paleness of her brow, and the way the dawn cast a glow over her cheeks. He wanted to remember her like this, brushed by gentle sunlight, long after he was gone.

With a slight bounce and a lift of her chin, she said, "Well, I'm going away, too." She dropped the satchel by her feet. "I'll be spending some time with a local family. I tried to find you last night to tell you, but you weren't at the stables. Then Etienne got angry at me, and—"

"Angry?"

"It's nothing." She shrugged it off. "I made arrangements for him to stay on the convent grounds rather than join me. This is for his own good, though he isn't happy about being left behind. We've rarely been apart, and he very much likes the family I'm spending the winter with—"

"The whole winter?"

She nodded. "The family's got a new babe coming and a toddler barely out of diapers. Weather will soon stop travel, so I'll be there at least until spring." She plucked at her skirts, shoulders rising as she drew in a deep breath. "It seems, Theo…it's time to say good-bye."

The speech he'd planned gathered in his throat, a tumble of words wishing her the best, thanking her for her kindness, none of which he could push past his lips. His planned farewell sounded weak and lifeless in his mind, too shaky to hold the weight of the feelings he had for her. As the river's current washed rhythmically against the keel of the canoe behind him, he dropped his gaze from her eyes and focused instead on her trembling chin and the flex of her pale throat.

What came out was, "I don't want to say goodbye."

Upon the raised berm, she stilled.

It was a reckless thing to say. He knew he should turn away, climb into the canoe, paddle to midriver, remove himself from temptation. But the soles of his boots shot roots into the ground. He wanted to stand here long enough to see the rosy light turn pale pink and then golden as it glazed her cheeks. He wanted to climb the berm and kiss her in the full sight of anyone awake early enough to see.

"Let's not say farewells." She raised pale, slim hands, palms out. "Let's just go our separate ways as if we'll both be back here, someday."

The lump in his throat swelled to giant proportions. The blond tresses of her hair danced around her face. He decided he would not be the first to move, because then he could watch as she walked away. Maybe then he would be able to sever the connection thrumming between them, here in the open air, amid the chill wind and the rosy dawn that marked a wistful ending.

"Every moment with you," he heard himself saying, "feels like stolen time."

A strangled little sound came from her. She pulled her lower lip between her teeth.

"You'd best leave first." He squinted down the riverbank but focused on nothing. "Just…go."

She glanced to her right and then to her left, took a step in one direction, only to turn to the other and then stop where she'd begun.

"You—you have to go first," she stuttered, spreading her arms. "No one has come with my canoe yet."

"If it's Etienne you're waiting for, you'll be here for a while." This very morning, Theo had placed the sleeping baby porcupine on an empty burlap sack beside the boy, a good-bye gift of a sort. He'd always respected the boy's urge to protect Cecile, but that same protectiveness had cratered any possibility of a better relationship. Now Theo had no time to rectify the situation. "He was dead asleep less than an hour ago."

"Etienne isn't taking me there. It's one of the many things we argued about."

He frowned. "Then who is paddling you downstream?"

"Sister Martha told me she'd send one of the laborers."

A tendril of suspicion curled in him, tightening as he looked across the wide, lush field of grass and saw not a single soul moving—no one but the two of them, alone on the bank at dawn. His ribs tightened. The Reverend Mother hadn't said anyone would be joining him on the canoe trip east…but the nun tended to let things work themselves out.

With a jump of his pulse, he asked, "Where, precisely, are you going?"

"To the Girards'."

The name hit him like one of Jules's left hooks. "Captain Girard."

She nodded. "My friend Marie's husband."

"They've got a *seigneurie* downstream, on the left bank."

"Yes." Her eyes narrowed. "You met Marie in Montreal yesterday."

"She's having a baby." He planted his hands on his hips as the pieces came together. "And her husband wants me to advise him about building a church in stone on his land."

Her face paled to the same white as the rabbit fur edging the hood of her cloak. Her head swiveled as she glanced up and down the empty bank, in search of another canoe to contradict his conclusion. Irritation was his first feeling, annoyance at the Reverend Mother's carelessness—or ignorance—in throwing them together like this. But that discomfort faded fast.

Now they would have more stolen time.

Suddenly he felt like a ship long languishing in the sea just as a fresh wind filled its sails.

"Come on board, Cecile." He turned back to the canoe to hide a rush of enthusiasm. "It's a long ride."

Sitting in the birchbark vessel, her satchel at her feet, Cecile pulled the furred edges of her cloak around her. She was thankful that Theo sat *behind* her, dragging the paddle through the black water. That way he couldn't see how emotional she'd become in his presence, remembering the way he'd looked at her when he'd said *Every moment with you feels like stolen time.*

Sitting in silence, but for the paddle gurgling through the water, felt like one endless moment, swelling with longing.

"About Captain Girard," came Theo's voice, suddenly, from behind her. "What can you tell me about him?"

It was a nonsense question, but she supposed he'd been trying to think up a neutral topic of conversation. The query brought her back into herself, her booted feet on the floor of the canoe, the river current rippling under the birchbark, the world outside her dreams.

"Lucas was a soldier of the Carignan-Salières Regiment several years ago. Before that, he fought in Flanders." When she thought of Captain Girard, the first thing that came to mind was how powerfully, and intimately, he looked at Marie when he believed no one was watching. She wasn't about to tell Theo that. "When the captain came back from his post in the wilderness, he was granted a large landholding, but only if he agreed to marry first."

"Marry a King's Girl. Your friend."

"Yes."

When Marie had told her the details of the courtship, Cecile had been left gaping. Marie's captain had wanted the land, but he hadn't been keen about forcing a King's Girl into the hard life of a settler. So, he'd made a deal with Marie, who hadn't wanted to marry either. The captain promised if she spent a winter with him as his wife, until the landholding was secured, then in the spring, he'd give her what she had wanted most—passage back to Paris.

For an entire Quebec winter, Captain Girard hadn't touched Marie—until she desperately wanted him to.

"He has a lovely stone cabin," she added, wincing once again at all the love she would never have. "It's the only stone cabin I know of, this far west of Quebec."

"Odd that he didn't build in wood. But smart, considering the risk of fire."

"I suppose." What silliness were they talking about? Cecile glanced up at the sky, scudding with gray-bottomed clouds. It seemed blasphemous, almost, to waste this stolen time on useless chatter. "Theo, what will you do first, once you're free?"

The paddle hit the surface of the water with a gentle splash.

"I've saved up some beaver pelts over the years, doing odd jobs on the days I was sent to Montreal. I suppose the first thing I'll do is trade them in for a better shirt and a new pair of boots."

She nodded, understanding the urge. Once Eduard had been out of her and Etienne's life, and before the creditors had caught up with her, she'd gone on a little splurge with the jar money long forbidden to her. It had felt good to put a proper waistcoat on Etienne's back, and slip herself into a lace-edged cambric chemise unstained by the blood of her wounds.

"And after the new boots?" Her heart squeezed. "What's next? Will you get blind drunk in some tavern?"

"Is that what you'll do if Talon discovers that you are, indeed, a widow?"

She startled enough to jolt off the seat a bit, and then chided herself for being surprised he knew such details. She had told him, on his first day as overseer, that her husband had been absent and she considered herself a widow. And now, with investigators in Montreal asking pointed questions, her degrading story was probably the big topic of conversation in all the taverns.

"I will *not* pick up a bottle." She shook her head hard. "Eduard was a drunkard. I won't mirror his stupidity."

"Smart woman."

"But I will be relieved," she confessed, "when I'm deemed by law to be unmarried, and can finally have some peace in this world."

Fingers crossed that Talon's investigation unearths no more than that.

"You don't have to join a convent to find that peace," Theo ventured. "You could sail away from these settlements and leave everything behind."

Breath gathered in her throat. Could this be his way of asking her to join him to go to France? She had considered the possibility, wondering if his feelings for her were as strong as her feelings for him. But it didn't matter. All was vanity—going to France was out of the question.

She swiveled on the bench, lifting her legs to settle them on the other side so she could face this man. She needed to meet his green gaze squarely when she answered such a weighty question.

"Theo." *My darling man.* "Do you remember when I asked why you hadn't escaped from indentured servitude to disappear into the wilderness?"

He nodded. The memory of their kiss by the riverbank rose like a wisp between them.

"Family obligations, you told me." She gathered courage to speak honestly, even while he looked at her with such intensity. "For those same reasons, I must stay here in the settlements."

A strange ripple passed across his face. "Etienne."

"Yes." Pained, she turned her head to peruse the riot of autumn color on the south bank of the river. "I love my son to the marrow of my bones. Never would I cross a sea and leave him behind. Nor would I tear him from the only home he's ever known. Nor take him to a place where he might never see anyone like himself again."

Theo leaned forward with an understanding nod, before paddling with more force than ever.

"And despite both our experiences, isn't it still a beautiful country?" She dropped her gaze to her gloved hands, daring in a quiet way to probe his own commitment to leaving. "Do you remember how soft and blue the snow can seem in the depths of winter? Or what it feels like, to draw a gentle frost into your lungs? And look at those flaming maples and golden beech trees and rust-leaved oaks. Won't you miss this, even a little bit?"

A smile tweaked his lips. "I'll miss only one thing when I leave here, Cecile. And that's you."

Though a flock of geese cawed above in the sky, and wisps of river fog curled up from the water, and the scent of a wood fire billowed from her shawl…the world went still again. Time stretched and stretched and stretched until the words from her heart found their way to her lips.

"I'll miss you, too, Theo."

What else was there to say, truly? The mutual acknowledgment of affection brought a tightening of her insides, but also a fresh calm. Acceptance, she supposed, and a trill of some finer feeling that stretched between them. She wasn't alone in her adoration. Theo found her worthy of his regard. With nothing left to be said, she swung her legs back over the bench so she could let bittersweet tears flow.

The voyage continued in a silence that she compared to the sacred quiet of a vaulted church. The canoe, pushed by the current as well as the paddle, cut swiftly through the water. Now and again, Theo pointed out a sight of interest—a buck lowering his antler rack as he drank at the water's edge, the silver flash of a sturgeon swimming by in the black waters. She acknowledged each sight with a nod or a little sound in her throat. She didn't dare open her mouth. To speak again would churn up new ripples, set loose fresh tears.

As the sun passed its zenith, Theo paused paddling. With his paddle, he pointed to a clearing ahead on the southern bank.

"That must be the Girards' landing."

"It is." How raw her voice. "I can just see the cabin through the trees."

While Cecile subtly wiped her face free of tears, Theo used the paddle as a rudder to cut the keel free of the current. Dragging hard, he urged the prow of the canoe toward the muddy bank until the cabin came fully into view.

Light spilled from the windows, though the day was bright. The promised warmth made her realize how cold she was, despite the layers of clothing she'd wrapped around herself. As the keel scraped into the mud, Theo leapt out into the shallows with a muscular grace. Gripping the prow, he dragged the canoe farther up the bank until it was secure.

She stood as he approached, bracing herself for the feel of his hands on her body. The padding of her coat and clothing should have dulled the pressure of his grip, but when he reached out, she felt the firm impression of every finger. He lifted her high. She flattened her hands on his broad shoulders. Their eyes locked as the ground shifted. The contours of his face—high cheekbones, hollows beneath, a sharp length of jaw, a rippled brow—so familiar, so very dear. On her dying day, she would remember how a good man had fixed her with his green gaze as he held her aloft.

She hardly felt the ground when he finally placed her there. He did not let go, but gripped her tighter.

"I have more to say." His voice was rough, as if dragged over gravel. "I should have said it in the canoe. Now I don't know if I'll get another chance."

Breath gathered in her chest.

"You are brave, Cecile. You have an enormous heart. I don't know how it fits inside someone so small. Don't let anyone break it. Don't let anyone break *you*."

Did she say his name out loud, or did it catch against the lump in her throat?

"You deserve happiness." He gave her a gentle shake. "Do you hear me?"

Yes, she could hear him. Yes, she nodded, blinking at a fresh wave of tears.

"I wish," he said, pushing the words out, "I wish—"

A shout interrupted him, though she didn't know what was shouted or from whence it came.

The shout repeated, closer.

"Cecile!"

A mountainous shape approached fast. Theo released his grip and stepped back a distance that felt like miles.

"Thank God you're here!"

Captain Girard came to a heavy running stop, coatless, hatless, his gray gaze panicked.

"The baby," he blurted as he swung an arm back toward the cabin. "It's coming—it's coming *now*."

CHAPTER SIXTEEN

Theo remained on the riverbank as Cecile, her blue skirts kicking up sun-bleached petticoats, tore full speed toward the Girards' cabin. The captain—despite his immense size—bolted after her. Theo stared at the place where Cecile had just stood as the thousand words he'd meant to speak choked him.

He'd waited too long.

He shook himself, mentally and physically. This was not the time nor the place to be dwelling on his own distress. An emergency unfolded at the cabin, and he must offer what help he could. Turning to the canoe, he grabbed one of the packets Mother Superior had ordered him to deliver—clean linens and medicines—probably meant for the birth, he realized. He raced up the muddy path, watching Cecile fly up the three stairs to swing the cabin door open. She twirled in the doorway and shut the door in the captain's face.

When Theo reached the porch a few moments later, the captain still stood at the door like a soldier at attention. Theo slung the package off his shoulder, set it on the floorboards, and raised his voice to let Cecile know he'd brought supplies and that they waited outside. Straightening, he slapped the captain's shoulder in sympathy, having no idea what else to do.

"It's a damnable thing," Captain Girard said between clenched teeth. "A *damnable* thing, what women suffer through."

Theo nodded, though he knew nothing about the matter. When his younger sisters and brothers had been born, Theo's stepfather had shuttled him off to a neighbor's house, saying it was bad luck to have another man's child anywhere near the birth of his own. By the time Theo's sisters had grown old enough to be married and birth nieces and nephews, Theo had already been exiled.

Just another item on a long list of losses.

A twisted, agonized cry erupted from inside the cabin. Captain Girard made a guttural noise and squeezed his eyes shut. At another eruption of pain, the giant turned on one heel and bolted to the far end of the porch.

Theo couldn't blame the man for wanting to disappear into the vast woods beyond. But as soon as the captain reached the porch's end, he swiveled on a heel and bolted back, repeating the pacing with ever more energy.

At one turn, the captain paused and blinked at Theo, as if seeing him for the first time.

"The Reverend Mother sent me," Theo said by introduction. "I'm Theo Martin, stonemason."

Awareness passed across that battle-hardened face. "You must be thirsty." The captain strode toward an upright crate and seized the wine bottle waiting on top of it. "I intended this for…after. But the birth is taking too long."

Pulling the cork out with a small knife he pulled from his belt, the captain poured wine into a pewter cup with a shaky hand before shoving the cup and a good portion of the wine into Theo's chest. As Theo raised the cup to his lips, the captain took a swig directly from the bottle, muscular throat flexing.

"The last babe came so fast, I missed this part." He swiped his chin with the back of his hand. "Women say the first babe takes the longest. Everyone told me not to worry, so back then, I came whistling home on the day she went into labor. When I got here, she was all cleaned up with our son in her arms."

The giant wasn't looking at him, wasn't really talking to him, and Theo got the impression he wasn't thinking about anything but his wife groaning behind these walls. The size of the man struck him. Theo was used to being the tallest person in any room, but he had to tilt his chin to meet this captain's tormented gaze. A soldier of the bloody wars of Flanders, Cecile had said. He was a wall of muscle who now flinched at every cry coming from within the cabin.

"I think," the captain said in a voice as sharp as chips of stone, "she didn't want me to witness this."

"No woman wants her husband to hear this, I imagine." Into Theo's mind came an image of Cecile lying on a bed, drenched in sweat, her belly a dome, her head thrown back in a cry of agony just like the one now vibrating through these stone walls…

His heart thudded. His hip hit the railing.

"I've seen war," the captain said, taking another swig. "Ugly, brutal slaughter. But I had a sword in hand. I could protect my own. This is not the same."

The captain's wife groaned anew. The giant swiveled on a heel for another lap of the porch.

Theo, draining the dregs in his cup, cast about for a way to distract him. "Your firstborn son," he asked. "Where is he now?"

"He's off with Oskanutú—a friend who winters here—about a mile away." His massive chest rose and fell. "I brought Charles there when I went to fetch Oskanutú's wife to help Marie." He glared toward what must be the cabin's bedroom at the far end. "I shouldn't have brought her to Montreal yesterday. I should have prepared for this sooner. My firstborn came a few weeks early, too."

Theo twisted the cup against the porch railing as the groans and grunts came quicker.

"A church," the captain blurted, rubbing his brow as he passed Theo on another lap of the porch. "Mother Superior sent you here to talk to me about raising a stone church."

"She did." Theo frowned as the boards beneath the captain's feet squealed. It occurred to him that if he and the captain could hear *her* cries, then perhaps the poor woman could also hear her husband wearing a furrow in the floorboards. "Captain—let's step off the porch."

"I'm not leaving until—"

A floorboard popped under his weight. The captain stopped in his tracks, glaring as if it had offended him. Then he settled the bottle of wine on the cask and descended the three stairs. Theo set his cup aside and followed.

"My hospitality is lacking, lad." The captain stopped in the clearing close enough to still hear what was going on, but far enough away not to be heard. "I don't usually greet guests like this."

"I'm no visiting dignitary, Captain."

"Lucas," he corrected. "No formalities necessary, especially when you're seeing me half mad. Best call me Lucas."

Theo tilted his head. "Theo."

"She's extraordinary, you know." Lucas grasped his hands behind his back, an act that made his barrel chest swell. "If it were me suffering in there and her out here greeting you, she would somehow have had you fed and watered while still changing the fever towels on my brow. But, never mind, you'll see what a fine lady she is, once she recovers." Lucas couldn't pull his gaze from the back window of the cabin, covered from the inside by an oilcloth. "She'll recover quickly, too. She's such a strong woman in every way, a true Québécoise."

Like Cecile.

The groans from the cabin became fainter but longer and then slid into an ominous silence. The captain stilled like a deer hearing the crack of a branch in the woods. A few minutes later, the door to the cabin swung open. Cecile, bereft of her cloak and hood and gloves, tresses tumbling from the roll of her hair, stepped outside, bearing a smile that beamed light in their direction.

"Congratulations, Captain Girard," she called as she hefted the bundle in her arms. "You're the father of a healthy baby girl."

"A daughter!" The captain clutched his heart. "And—and my wife?"

"Out of breath." Cecile laughed. "But utterly triumphant."

Even giants could move fast, for Lucas reached the porch in a blur. Beside the giant, Cecile looked the size of a corn-husk doll. When the captain crouched to take the babe into his own arms, she hefted the swaddled bundle and settled the covered head of the newborn against the ball of the captain's arm. Cecile's smile for the baby went tremulous as she released the infant into the captain's arms.

Theo's heart beat against bone. Cecile glowed with happiness for her friend, but he saw something more in her expression. A yearning. A yawning hunger. She wanted a babe of her own.

He'd known it from the first—Cecile did not belong in a convent.

How he ached to be the one to give her a child. A thousand images tumbled behind his eyes. Of him standing where Lucas now stood, taking a warm babe from Cecile's arms. Except it was Cecile's babe peeking out from the swaddling clothes. It was Cecile's face pink from exertion, with that same beaming smile, but brighter. All the words he'd been so eager to tell her distilled into one undeniable truth.

He was in love with Cecile Tremblay.

CHAPTER SEVENTEEN

Cecile's hands still trembled as she gathered the bloody linens from around the cabin's one bedroom and tossed them in a sack for laundering. She kept a keen eye on Marie, lying under fresh covers, her dark hair damp from sweat. It had been a little more than an hour since the birth, long enough to get Marie cleaned up, bound in dressings, and her hair combed into a neat plait. Still, her friend didn't sleep, her eyes fluttering half open and then drifting closed again, a saint's smile fixed upon her face.

"Will she be all right?" Cecile whispered to the Huron midwife—Hateya—now returning a bewildering array of medicinal herbs and mosses to her reed basket. "There was so much blood."

"No more blood than usual." Hateya nodded at a dozing Marie with affection. "She's very strong. You have children?"

Cecile shook her head with a wince. In truth, this was the first birth she'd ever seen. When she'd been married, her husband had forbidden her to leave the grounds of his cabin, purposely isolating her from the other women and the entire community of Trois-Rivières. Nor had he wanted more children. One hungry little mouth was enough, he'd said, referring to Etienne. But it wasn't until now, having held Marie's warm-from-the-womb daughter against her chest, that she realized the full extent of the joy Eduard had stolen from her.

"I will come again tomorrow." Hateya slipped the handle of the medicine basket up to her elbow, the pale pink shells around her neck clinking. "The after pains will begin soon." Hateya nodded to a cup on a side table. "Give her that to drink when they do."

"And the babe…" Currently being rocked in Captain Girard's arms in the other room. "Is there something I must do for her?"

"When her daughter cries for milk, Marie will take her up."

The Huron woman nodded and left, closing the door behind her. Through that door, Cecile heard Captain Girard's rumbling voice and words spoken in the Huron tongue.

Theo must be in the parlor, too, and the thought was a jolt. Since her arrival here, time had been a blur, but Cecile remembered the beautiful words he'd spoken to her by the banks of the river.

Marie murmured, "Ceci?"

She hurried to Marie's bed and plopped down into the cane chair set beside it. Her friend lay back on the pillows but could barely keep her eyelids open.

"I'm so glad"—Marie patted the linens until she found Cecile's hand—"that you made it here in time."

"Barely." Cecile gripped Marie's hand, damp from washing. "You were fighting to push her out when I stepped into the room."

"All the hours before were boring, just me pacing and complaining." Marie shifted her head on the pillow, forcing her eyes open. "Did it terrify you?"

"Absolutely."

Marie laughed, her beautiful gaze weary but suffused with joy. "But it was miraculous, wasn't it?"

Cecile ducked her head and nodded. If Marie's breasts were not so swollen, Cecile would have laid her head on Marie's chest, slung her arms around her, and hugged her tight. She was so relieved Marie had made it through.

"How is Lucas faring?" Marie asked. "I fear we'll have to replace the porch floorboards after all his pacing."

"He's fine. *He* didn't just birth a child." Cecile remembered, as Lucas entered the room, how he'd bent over Marie to run his hands through her hair, whispering words so loving that Cecile had found herself overwhelmed by the intimacy. "Right now, he's in the other room, sitting by the hearth, rocking your daughter who is sleeping. As you should be."

"I'd love to, but the after pains are starting." Marie winced as she slid her free hand over the covers above her somewhat-deflated abdomen. "Talk to me, Cecile. Distract me."

"Drink this first." Cecile swept up the cup of medicine that Hateya had brewed and, lifting Marie's head, held it to her friend's lips.

Marie drank it down and made a face. "Just as bitter as I remember. I don't understand why I can't add maple syrup to the brew." She winced, trying hard to swallow away the bad taste. "Tell me, did that pirate of a stonemason come with you today? I thought I heard his voice on the porch."

"Yes, he's here." Cecile put the cup back on the bedside table and gave Marie a hard eye. "Was it you who planned it, having both of us come here together?"

"Ceci, what a suspicious mind you have." Marie widened her eyes in an exaggerated way. "Didn't Mother Superior make the travel arrangements?"

"My goodness." Cecile leaned closer to her friend as realization dawned. "You saw Sister Martha just yesterday. You two set this up together."

"Not exactly. I mean, I did ask Sister Martha to send Theo here. But I only joked about how nice it would be for you to come at the same time. Because you hadn't agreed to spend the winter with me yet." Marie shifted her shoulders against the pillow, her smile turning puckish. "In any case, I'm thrilled you both made it here. After witnessing the lightning arcing between you two yesterday, I did wonder if having you both in the same canoe would set it on fire."

"Goodness, Marie, listen to you." Cecile tried to stop the flush, but it swept over her. "Is there even a plan for a stone church, or is that a ruse, too?"

"Not a ruse, just a convenient excuse." Marie winced as another spasm gripped her, held, and then released. "Lucas and I have been discussing the matter for some time."

"Well, your plans—both of them—are doomed to failure." Cecile sighed at her friend's audacity. "Theo is going back to France in just a few weeks. So, he won't be building your stone church, nor spending any more time with me."

Marie's brow rippled. "But you're in love with him."

Cecile ducked her head. Damn Marie and those all-seeing eyes.

She definitely felt something.

Could it be love?

"Ceci, I know you have feelings for that man." Marie twisted a little on the bed to better face her. "Don't you dare deny it—not to me and not anymore. For too long, I denied my feelings for Lucas. That didn't make them go away. I only found happiness after I came to understand and accept—"

"Please stop." Cecile pulled away, for every word out of Marie's mouth felt like a pike through her gut. "I won't deny that I'm drawn to him. Strongly." A prickling showered over her, a thousand tickling needles, as she thought about Theo looming over her only a few hours ago, his mouth shaping the words *you deserve to be happy.* "But…I've never experienced love, Marie. I'm not even sure what it looks like."

But she did, she realized, as she gazed down at a woman still suffering from the birth of a beautiful baby girl. Despite the pain, Marie glowed with joy and contentment. In the other room sat her loving husband, who'd nearly gone mad with worry during the birth.

"Is it a passion for him, then?" Marie's brow rippled with confusion. "Is that what the lightning is all about?"

Heat blazed up from under Cecile's bodice. Really, why were they having this conversation?

"Passion is a wonderful thing." Marie squeezed her hand. "If that's what's drawing you to Theo, you should accept that, too, acknowledge it, even embrace it. Especially after all you've suffered with—"

"Shouldn't you be sleeping by now?" Cecile fussed with the sheets, desperate to end this conversation.

"Don't let fear stop you from loving." Marie went still, then breathed through another cramp. "Most of all," she continued, as the cramp slowly abated, "don't let that bastard of a husband ruin your life anymore. You deserve to be happy."

Overcome at the same words Theo had spoken to her, she turned away from Marie to stare blindly toward the oilskin-covered window.

"Explore all those confusing feelings," Marie persisted. "Listen to the natural pull of your body."

"Please tell me you didn't say any of this to Sister Martha while you both were meddling."

"Oh, my darling Ceci, Sister Martha understands the world better than you think."

She planted her head in her hands, groaning. To have such a friend as this was the greatest gift—Cecile had once helped Marie defy a king all those years ago—and yet, now Cecile wished she could stop Marie from talking.

"Enough, Marie." She straightened with a long exhale. "All this talk is futile. I told you, there is no future for Theo and myself."

"I'm not talking about the future." Marie's eyelids fluttered as the medicine began to take hold. "I've done my part to get you together…the rest is up to you."

"The rest of *what?*"

"The parlor," Marie murmured. "That's where you'll be sleeping."

"I know. Lucas set up a pallet for me. Now what—"

"While you're in the parlor," Marie interrupted, "Theo will be sleeping in the barn. Lucas and I will be here in this bed, behind a closed door, deaf and mute to anything but a baby's cry."

At the implication, Cecile went prickly warm, though the fire in the hearth had banked to coals and needed another log. "Heavens, Marie. To think that you were raised in a convent."

"Don't worry…about pregnancy." Marie tugged on the blanket, her eyes sliding closed as she fought exhaustion. "A man as handsome as that…must have plenty of experience in avoiding—"

"Saints alive." Cecile bolted to her feet. "Your pain is making you delirious."

"I want you happy, Ceci."

Those words again. Of course she wanted to be happy. But she'd never found any joy in the marriage bed. And to lie in a bed with Theo—whether he gave her joy or not—would make parting from him only more difficult.

"This conversation is over." Cecile headed to the door. "You get some sleep, Marie."

"I'll try…But I hope you don't sleep at all."

Marie's fading laughter followed her out of the room.

CHAPTER EIGHTEEN

With the burnt end of a piece of tinder, Theo scratched another black mark on the barn wall, a tally of how long he'd been at the Girards'.

He calculated carefully.

One more day to freedom.

Sitting by the iron stove, he tossed the tinder into the fire and waited for a rush of liberation to blast through him. For four years, he'd been anticipating the day he would step onto a ship as a free man, a ship whose billowed sails would transport him across a sea to where he belonged. With every cut of a whip on his back, he'd vowed to return to the family he'd left behind.

Now here he was, with a belly full of moose steak, sitting in Captain Girard's barn on the shores of the Saint Lawrence River, his mind not on the trip home, but on thinking up ways to stretch the final hours so the memories of Cecile would last a lifetime.

The door to the barn swung open, letting in the howl of the wind as well as the icy bite of a storm. A figure appeared out of the darkness. He blinked once, twice, to clear his vision. Firelight illuminated a small, slim silhouette. Mentally, he shook himself. More than once, he'd dreamed of her coming to him in the night.

Despite all his blinking, the image remained, resolving into the shape of the woman he couldn't stop dreaming of.

Why are you here?

He wanted to ask the question, anticipating an answer such as, *Can you fix the hinge on the cabin door?* Or, *The fire has gone out in the parlor, and I don't want to bother Marie or the captain to re-light it,* even while aching to hear different words such as, *I want you, Theo.*

I love you.

Shooting to his feet, he reached for his deerskin coat hanging on a peg pounded into the wall. Swinging it around his shoulders, he said, "The captain needs me?"

"No." Cecile's breathy voice was stolen by the wind as she pushed the door closed behind her. "Everyone is sleeping. Even the baby—swaddled and lulled by the wind."

The tendons in her throat pulled so tight they formed a V. Something was wrong. It took all his will not to step toward her, draw her close, and whisper, *Everything will be all right.*

I promise.

She ventured a step into the circle of firelight. "The captain told me you're leaving tomorrow."

He swayed back a fraction. Had she come to say goodbye? He wouldn't be able to do that without kissing her one more time—now that they were alone. And if he kissed her, he wouldn't be able to stop.

"This storm is the start of winter." He tossed his coat back onto the peg. "Better to leave tomorrow, or I'll be here for the whole season."

He should have departed a week ago. He'd come to the Girards to talk about building a stone church, but every time he'd broached the subject, Lucas had been understandably distracted. There was no reason for Theo to stay. But his sentence was winding down, and damn it, he didn't *want* to leave. So, he'd stolen more time, earning his keep by chopping wood, mending fences, and helping to paint a new coat of pitch on two of the Girards' canoes.

Because that's what a lovesick fool did.

"I wish I was leaving here, too." She tugged at the edges of her oversized shawl. "Marie is healthy and out of childbed. She and Lucas know what they're doing. I'm…I'm just in the way."

She was lying. Theo knew the Girards needed her. He'd seen how much Cecile helped. He'd once come around the edge of the house, carrying wood, and found Cecile sitting on the porch. She'd hummed as she rocked the swaddled bundle in her arms. He couldn't pull his eyes away from her, and didn't have to, for she was oblivious to anything but the babe, her face a rictus of tearful joy and agony.

He'd yearned to approach her, wipe the streak of flour from her cheek, pull a tress of hair from across her brow, and slip the pad of his thumb into the hollow of her throat. There were other urges, too—to haul her into his arms and kiss her senseless and give her a babe of her own. Stronger than even that was the ache to pull her head against his chest, to murmur in her ear that she deserved better than what life had served her, to tug the pins from her hair and let it tumble down her back just so he could run his fingers through it.

Instead, he'd stayed where he stood, tightening his grip on the load of firewood in his arms. He felt like one of the sailors in a Greek book he'd once read, who had tied themselves to the masts of their ship to resist the pull of the sirens.

He felt that way now, standing across from her in the silence of the barn. "The Girards still need you here, Cecile. Don't go back to the convent."

"The convent?" She laughed softly, but not with humor. "I can't go back there. Not anymore."

His senses came alert.

"Oh…I should have told you." A gust slipped through the boards to set loose a strand of blond hair from her plait. "Despite all my pleas, Sister Martha has refused to take me in as a novice."

Her deep gaze, with its swirling currents, fixed on him—and stayed and stayed, draining his strength. He'd been convinced she would never become a nun. Yet he'd respected her insistence and allowed it to be a shield thrown up against him. Now she stood before him as vulnerable as he'd ever seen her, wearing next to nothing and saying she would never join a convent.

"Cecile." The wind howled around the boards of the barn as another wall between them tumbled down. "Go back to the cabin."

"I don't want to." She sucked in a quick breath. "We have so little time."

She loosened her grip on the shawl and let it drop. Underneath, she wore the most gossamer of shifts. The firelight penetrated the fabric, revealing the outlines of her legs and hips and the shadowy juncture between. In his mind he took a step back from temptation, but his feet did not comply.

"I'll never see you again, after tomorrow." She stepped out of the pool of the discarded shawl and approached within arms' reach. "I'll never get another chance to kiss you again, Theo."

He laid his fingertips over her mouth, but his name had already passed through her lips. Wet and warm, those lips, swelling against his fingertips. The walls of the room bowed around him. All his efforts to interpret her words as something other than what he longed for failed.

Just a kiss, he told himself.

She tasted of wine. He drank his fill with his nose pressed against the soft pillow of her cheek. Wine had been fortification, no doubt, to propel her to this barn. He wondered how long she'd paced in the cabin, contemplating coming to him.

He nudged her lips open, though he knew he should move slowly and gently. But his mind vaulted forward to when his hips would be between her thighs. To when her bottom would fill his palms as he drove himself into her.

She made a startled gasp against his mouth as if she felt his mental thrusts.

Just before the point of drowning completely, he pulled away and seized hold of his better self.

"Don't stop," she sputtered, throwing her arms around his neck. "I want… I want…"

"I know what you want. I want you, too." With one hand, he tugged at the rawhide tie that secured the end of her braid. Plunging his fingers between the braided sections, he loosened the luxurious softness until her hair unfurled down her back. "You should never bind your hair." He combed his fingers through it, down, down, down. "Not in front of me."

A little convulsion shuddered through her, lips parting in breathy surprise. Had her husband never told her how lovely she was?

Of course he hadn't, the fool.

"I used to watch you from where I stood on the scaffolding," he confessed, teasing her with a kiss on the jaw and then at one corner of her lips. "Especially as you drifted in and out of the schoolhouse to lay the dinner table. You walk like a ship sailing in a breeze. I couldn't take my eyes off you."

Her eyes shimmered.

"For so long," he said, pulling her against him, "I've wanted you in my arms like this."

"And I, you."

The sound was breathy, full of wonder, and hit him with gale force. This feeling between them was madness, sure to end in tears, but he knew that this loving was going to happen tonight.

"I'll give you everything you want, Ceci." He spoke against her cheek. "I'll give you what you don't even know you want."

Tonight, he would make their loving unforgettable.

CHAPTER NINETEEN

Had she ever really lived?

The thought rose like a spark from a campfire, winking out before Cecile could gather the mental clarity to seek an answer. There would be time enough for contemplation later. Right now, delicious sensation rippled through her body everyplace where their bodies touched, convening on a low ache that only Theo could satisfy.

"The shift," he whispered. "Take it off."

She did as he bade, seizing handfuls of the cambric. As she lifted it, the warmth coming from the iron stove painted the side of her leg higher and higher. She lost sight of Theo as she pulled the gathered fabric over her head, but she heard his intake of breath as she exposed herself and tossed the cloud of fabric away. Those eyes were as green as the shallows of the river where she and Etienne had once lived, calm waters reflecting sunlight.

Theo went speechless, a muscle in his cheek flexing, his Adam's apple bobbing, his breathing quickening.

Under that hungry perusal, she no longer felt an urge to hide herself or cower. She pulled her shoulders back, giving her breasts a prouder tilt as the nipples beaded into a tingling tightness. She swayed, silently willing him to lay his fingers upon the path his eyes had blazed.

As his gaze reached her hips, he paused and his expression darkened. She wondered why—and then flinched. She'd forgotten about the array of burn scars. There was no way to cover them when she was naked. A thought shot through her mind. *Please don't ask. Don't bring that monster into this room, into this sacred moment.*

She grasped Theo's hand, urged his fingers open, and placed his callused palm against her scarred hip.

"It was a long time ago. That's…over." She flattened her hand over his. "The scars are long healed."

"The physical ones are." He stretched his fingers to cover as many as he could. "But wounds as cruel as these must run deep."

He dropped to a knee, seized her hips, and replaced his hand with his lips. She held his shoulders for balance, quivering as he kissed each scar.

Once done, he shifted, pressing his forehead against her abdomen with a groan, kissing the button of her navel.

His fingers dug deeper into her hips. "I will never hurt you, Ceci."

"I know." She loved that he used the pet name. The sound of it chimed through her.

"No pain," he muttered. "Only pleasure."

Then he dipped his head—and his lips—lower.

The world spun. She threw her head back with a gasp. Her legs lost feeling—only the grip of his hands on her hips held her upright. She muffled the shout shooting up her throat, but a sound slipped out anyway, strangled and hardly human.

"They can't hear us at the cabin, not with the storm raging." He spoke the words against her body, and she could feel his warm breath on her tender inner thigh. "Make all the noise you want."

At his command, she dropped all attempts at control. As he resumed his wet kisses, hungry cries ripped up her throat, building with the wave of sensation uncoiling from the place where he was rolling his tongue, threatening to launch her senses beyond the rafters—beyond the stars.

And then, all of a sudden, *did.*

Sometime during the flight, he slid up to his feet. She collapsed in his arms as she floated down from the pleasure he'd given her. Slowly, she became aware of the scent of resinous pine and winter cold and cut maple clinging to his shirt, a male scent that filled her head as strength returned to her knees.

She tilted her head back to witness the triumphant smile he bestowed upon her. His river-green eyes gleamed bright, the fire lighting them gold. He pushed her hair off her brow and kissed the center of her forehead, and she wondered how she'd ever believed this gentle, beautiful man was a brute.

"As passionate as you are beautiful," he whispered, his fingers teasing her chin up. "Will you admit now that I was right about the convent?"

A laugh bubbled out of her.

It had always been a desperate idea.

"I may need more convincing," she teased, running a finger down the linen weave of his shirt. "Take this off."

A ripple passed over his face. "Ceci," he whispered, bending his head close. "Maybe we should—"

"The breeches, too."

A light flared in his eyes. His jaw shifted as he searched for words. "Think a moment. You know I'm leav—"

"I want more, Theo. I want everything."

His gaze flared. She glimpsed the hungry wolf behind his control and ached to see him as unleashed as she had been. She knew this delight would be only a night. She would savor every hour, every minute, and remember it for a lifetime.

Because this was more than passion.

This was Theo, the man she loved.

He tugged his shirt from the waistband of his breeches. She'd seen Theo shirtless on the scaffolding many times, trying in vain not to gape at his wide, gleaming shoulders. Now she saw up close the hard plates of his chest and the lines of demarcation on his abdomen. She gave in to her most primitive urge to run her fingertips over the ridges and valleys of those swellings.

Then she switched her fingers for her lips.

His chest and abdomen tightened against her mouth in a delightful, quivering way. His skin was so hot, a little salty. A faint spray of dark hair surrounded his flat nipples, to which she gave some attention. When he groaned, a thrill shimmied through her. Was one night going to be enough to explore him, to discover all the ways they could love?

With new boldness, she ran a finger into the groove that led to his navel, and then lower still, over the trail of dark hair.

He gripped her hand, stopping its progress.

She glanced up at him to find his eyes squeezed shut, his jaw tight, his lips pressed together. The rugged, raw beauty of his face showed the pleasure she was giving him. Her overworked heart made a ragged leap. To think she had such power.

He muttered, "I'll take off the breeches later."

When he opened his eyes, his gaze bordered on feral. With a dip, he slid an arm around her waist and thrust her up against him, coming in for a hard kiss, sealing their lips. Lifting her, he moved away from the warmth of the fire.

A breeze siphoned through the walls and slid over her naked body in ways that made her tingle. He leaned down and tossed her onto a pillow-and-blanket-strewn bed. With the firelight behind him, his face was half light, half shadow as he crouched beside her.

Her knees slid open—the boldness of that thrilled her. She ached for more than his kisses, but he slapped a hand on one of her knees to keep her still.

"We'll come to that." His breathing came harsh. "I want you to be ready."

"Theo—"

"Let me touch you. All over. Yes?"

Yes yes yes yes yes. She seized his hand, intending to place it on her breast, but he resisted her pull.

"I've a stonemason's hands." He opened his palm so she could see the calluses and ridges. "Mortar is caustic. It hardens the skin—"

"I'm not that delicate."

"In my eyes, you are." He moved to the stove to dip a linen in a water bucket close to the fire's warmth. He came back, slipped a hip on the pallet, and lay the damp linen against her collarbone.

"Too cold, too hot?"

The linen felt as warm as a kiss. "Perfect."

Flattening his hand behind the damp cloth, he swept it into the hollow of her throat and then along the line of one collarbone. She swallowed hard, a burn of eagerness twining with a prickle of anticipation.

The moisture left in its wake cooled her skin. He repeated the motion on her left side, drawing the same warm path over her neck with a gentle stroke. He lay the warm cloth upon her breast, and those strangled noises threatened in her throat again.

"You fit in my hand," he murmured, "so perfectly. Your breast belongs in my grip."

When he squeezed gently, she arched her back, driving her nipple against his palm. Her breasts felt heavy, full and tender—and more so, when Theo removed his hand to blow upon the damp fabric separating her skin from his tongue.

"Open your eyes," Theo commanded. "Look at me while I touch you."

Her eyelids were lead-heavy, but she did as he bade, watching him as he slid the cloth over her ribs, around the indentation of her waist, to linger for a moment on her lower belly, just below her navel.

He paused there, looking her over for a painfully long time. Her thighs trembled with new ferocity. She bent a knee, then laid it flat, only to bend the other, the ache growing and, at the same time, sharpening to a point. She slid her own hands under her back to prevent herself from reaching down to ease that ache. For she saw, stiff inside his breeches, the straining member he would fill her body with, before this night was over. In that way, Theo would bring her the pleasure she craved.

She wasn't sure she could wait.

"Theo."

As if on command, he slid the cloth lower, between her thighs, pressing his fingers into the ache. She arched against his touch as he moved in gentle strokes. Little bolts of lightning shot through her. She vibrated along with a crack of thunder outside. He increased the pressure so she felt, beyond the linen weave, the ridges of the calluses on the pads of his fingers, then she pressed her head against the pallet and shouted as she became, once again, a writhing creature of light and fire.

Sometime later, the moisture of the linen cloth cooling, she managed to blink her eyes open. Theo, with a hip on the pallet, bore an intense, wondrous expression on his face.

She stuttered, "D-did I… Did I scream?"

"A little." The corners of his eyes crinkled. "I'll be making you scream louder than that before this night is through."

She bit her lower lip, lost for words.

"Your skin flushes after your pleasure. You moan and throw your arms over your head." His brows twitched as he shook his head. "It's the most beautiful thing I've ever seen."

A weakness rippled through her, in body and spirit. Had he bathed her in warmed honey, she couldn't feel more treasured. She gathered what strength remained to rise to a sitting position so she could touch his jaw. How could it be that she would find a man who was kind, patient and loving when she had felt, for so long, forsaken by both God and man? Was she dreaming? Would she wake up?

How could she ever let him go?

"No more teasing." She surged close to his beautiful face and offered her lips. "I want you inside me."

CHAPTER TWENTY

I have nothing to offer you, Theo wanted to say. *You deserve better.*

His mind screamed those words, yet he had no power to retreat from her touch. She slipped her fingers along his jaw and then slid them deep into his hair. Her face, lit golden by the fire, pleaded for loving. Gilded hair tumbled over one shoulder to pool upon a naked thigh. Waves of scent came off that waterfall, of kitchen herbs and baby's milk.

All resistance crumbled into dust.

Her mouth moved sweetly under his. He pressed harder than he should, as he hadn't dared before. The sight of her scars was still branded in his mind—proof of the cruelty she'd suffered at another man's hands. Yet, as he coaxed her down, flat on the pallet, she didn't shudder or flinch. She parted her lips for a deeper kiss, gripped him by the arms, and guided him atop her. His body surged with a rush of power. How could it be that he'd come to be desired by a woman as passionate and brave as this?

He kissed her forehead, her eyes, her jaw, and her throat, worshipping more than just her lovely flesh. He honored the loving mother, the hard worker, the brave survivor. She deserved a prince, not a destitute indentured servant, or a stonemason with a criminal past, or a foolish man who'd been determined to leave her behind.

"Ah, Ceci." How he loved that little nickname. "You could ask me to slay a dragon, and I'd leave to find a sword."

A laugh rippled in her throat. "It's enough that you're here with me, Theo."

"Are you sure about this?"

She let one arm fall above her head, giving a lift to one soft, gorgeous breast. "How can you doubt it?"

Her half-lidded look was too hungry to ignore. He pushed off the pallet to unbutton his breeches, loosen his loincloth, and let the garments fall to the floor. He couldn't wait to plunge into her body, but the stronger urge was to *claim* her—*impregnate her*. But—no. He would stop that from happening, at least for now. In his mind, the whole world was changing. Before he could contemplate exactly how, Ceci beckoned him down.

He'd think about it later.

He straddled her.

Breathing hard, she ran a hand over his chest and abdomen, as she'd done before. His muscled body was the result of years of hard labor. She was rounded in all the right places. She sank her teeth into her lower lip as she explored even lower. He squeezed his eyes shut, reining in his pleasure as she gripped him.

In a whisper full of breathy humor, she said, "Am I hurting you?"

"No." He reached down to remove her fingers. "Explore later. I have a promise to keep."

He shifted his stance to nudge her thighs apart and settle his hips. She watched his every move with delighted eyes. Kneeing her legs farther apart, he pressed himself against her parting warmth.

I love you, Cecile.

He might have whispered the words aloud—he didn't know and he didn't care. All of his senses focused on the merging of their bodies, first gently, and then, after a breath, moving deeper into her. He leaned down to kiss her, drawing out those little noises she made as he set a rhythm according to her pleasure. Taut and ready, he was, but he wouldn't disappoint her. He thrust and thrust, her moans rising in pitch.

As she arched her back, he felt the small muscles inside her clench. Triumph rushed through his body. Teetering on the cliff's edge of his own banked climax, he witnessed her shuddering excitement, the ripples running through her, exciting him as well.

But he held—held—held—until, her pleasure slaked, he heaved himself back to sanity and slid himself out of her.

Release thundered through him, explosive and body-shaking. He threw his head back. Into his ecstasy slid a sliver of regret that he wasn't her husband, that he wasn't still inside her now.

Marry her.

The thought shot through him as he tumbled to her side. She rolled into him, all breathy and warm. Pulling her closer—*marry* her—he swept her silky hair across his waist and buried his face against her head. Running deeper than a vein of quartz in a mountain of granite was this love he had for Ceci.

She whispered, "Can I stay the night?"

He pulled away to glance down at her sleepy face, luminescent in the light of the stove fire. "I won't let you go."

"Good." She snuggled closer. "Dawn is hours and hours away."

"Dawn doesn't matter." He tightened his grip. "I won't let you go—not ever."

She ducked her chin. Not believing his words, perhaps. He couldn't blame her. He'd been convinced that separation was inevitable, and so, he knew, had she. Yet being together was inevitable. He knew this, now, to the very core of his soul.

"Ceci." He caught her jaw and coaxed it up, so she could see his new conviction—and believe it. "I love you too much to leave you."

CHAPTER TWENTY-ONE

She must be dreaming.

With her head cradled in the nook of Theo's shoulder, she looked up at the man who'd spoken magical words. Firelight limned his jaw and cheekbones and brightened the hollows of his eyes. She'd been memorizing his features all night, tucking away the images for when she'd be bereft forever.

I love you too much to leave you.

The words vibrated through her. But they couldn't be real. The intensity of the pleasure he'd gifted her had muddled her mind, made limp her body, and set loose desperate fantasies. Surely this was all an illusion, birthed from the ashes of broken dreams.

"You will…" She could barely move her tongue. "You will stay here in the settlements?"

"Yes." He huffed a breath, half wonder, half astonishment. "Yes, I will."

The future bloomed in her mind. Every night, the two of them entwined like this on the same bed. Every morning woken with a kiss. Every afternoon, he would return to their home. But just as her heart lifted in her chest, the old fears rose, too, pressing down hope.

"But…but you've been counting down the days." The images in her mind blurred. "Your family… They're expecting you to return home."

His gaze flickered and then drifted to the rafters. "They were expecting me, for a while. Years ago."

Under her ear, the rhythm of his heart intensified, and she felt a vein pulse against her jaw.

"The latest letter from home came from my younger brother." He raised his free arm and laid it across his brow. "He described the situation in a different way than my mother ever did in earlier years."

"Different?"

"Much has changed in my absence." His jaw tightened. "Many of the changes are good—in a way I never foresaw. My younger sisters are all married and settled. My youngest brother is no longer an apprentice, but a master mason, and he has plenty of work to support my stepfather and injured brother. If my mother was still living, I'd be tied in knots about staying in the settlements…but she's gone."

"Oh, Theo."

His throat flexed as he pulled her closer. "I miss her. And Guéret, and my step-siblings, and the band of masons. But now I can't deny a truth I've been avoiding. Benoit hinted at it in his letter. If I—forever a convict—rejoined the masons, my presence might destroy the prosperity that my brother has rebuilt in the years I've been gone."

His voice was somber, and her heart went sore. "Your brother said this?"

"Not plainly, but I heard the message."

"Are you sure you're not reading the letter wrong?"

"No. I'm seeing the situation clearly for the first time." His shoulders shifted under her. "My absence from Guéret is like a wound that has stitched over. If I returned, I'd rip it back open."

She lightly traced his chest with her fingernails. She knew she would do better to keep her mouth shut, stop asking questions, lest her probing made Theo change his mind about staying. But what kind of loving partner would she be, if she allowed Theo to make a sacrifice that he would regret later?

Her heart halfway up her throat, she asked, "And what of revenge?"

Theo sucked in a slow, long breath.

"The viscount did you such wrong." *Quiet, you fool!* "Doesn't it eat at you, that injustice? Wasn't vengeance another reason why you counted down the days to your freedom?"

The wind whistled around a corner of the cabin, rising and falling in pitch, as she waited in agony for an answer.

He sighed. "I can't deny that the idea of vengeance has kept me alive for a long time."

She drew her lower lip between her teeth. She understood all too well how plotting revenge could keep a soul sane in the face of horrors. With that grim thought, a dark wind cut through her, carrying icy memory and the weight of so many dangerous secrets.

"I think it was knowing *you* these past months that made me give up the idea of revenge." He planted a damp kiss against her temple, close to the scar Eduard had given her. "I've come to realize that if I went back and murdered the viscount, I would become exactly the kind of murderous criminal that the law had wrongly branded me. Think about that, Ceci—just witnessing your courage, your generosity, and your kindness was enough to wash the acid from my heart."

Oh, Theo. Tears sparked behind her eyes. *I'm not as kind or courageous as you believe.*

"Between Benoit's letter," he continued, "and being here with you, I've changed my mind about everything. I know what I need to do."

She clamped her jaw against the confession surging up her throat. The past was the past. What she'd done, she'd done—there was no taking it back. Telling Theo her ugly secret would be folly. Speaking of her crime would destroy their future before it had even begun.

But didn't Theo deserve to know what kind of woman now lay in his bed?

"Ceci, I want us to be so happy." His voice rippled with wonder. "I want to build a new life with you."

She squeezed her eyes shut, only to see the old nightmare unfurl upon the insides of her eyelids.

"A life," he forged on, "like this one the captain built for Marie. We'll have a home of our own, a warm hearth, a bit of land." He trailed a fingertip down her cheek only to stop under her chin to force her face up. "A thousand horses couldn't pull me away from you now."

The tears welling in her eyes blurred the beauty of his face, but not the sight of his joy. What kind of woman would keep a secret from such a man? How could they be happy amid a web of secrets and lies?

"Oh, Theo."

He pulled back a fraction, his gaze flickering.

"Would you still love me"—she whispered the words, choking on her breaking heart —"if I confessed that I murdered my husband?"

CHAPTER TWENTY-TWO

June, 1673

The sky was as blue as a marsh violet.

After Etienne left the cabin to hunt in the north pasture for small game, Cecile strode east into the woods, hoping to find some early-ripening berries or mushrooms. With a basket in the crook of her elbow and a flintlock slung across her back, she'd followed the banks of a tributary of the Saint Maurice River that spilled into the island-strewn headlands of the greater Saint Lawrence. The canopy of pine boughs cast a cool shade against a blazing sun that melted pine resin into a perfume that clouded the air.

Under her feet, the ground sank spongy after a week of rain, which she hoped would encourage the sprouting of orange-capped spruce boletes or—Etienne's favorites—chanterelles. She would add them to the rabbit stew simmering over embers back in the cabin. When the day's work was done, she and Etienne would eat together, just the two of them. Afterward, he would read aloud the stories of Gargantua and Pantagruel from the book Marie had lent her when they'd visited the Girards a few weeks ago.

Hearing a branch snap, she dropped her basket to the ground. Slinging the flintlock into her hands, she swung toward the noise. Bears and mountain lions and wolves roamed these woods, but what she glimpsed was a thousand times more dangerous. A man, loping along the riverbank, his face covered to the eyes with a ratty, unkempt beard.

Recognition shot through her like a hot lead plug.

"Put that down, woman." Her husband's teeth flashed as he stopped, planting the butt of his own rifle on the carpet of pine needles. "Your man is home."

His voice funneled ice down her spine. Just at the sight of him, she felt the rippled scars on her hip tighten. Her right shoulder ached in remembrance of an old dislocation. Pain throbbed in the divot at her temple, where he'd struck her with a pewter tankard. The terrors seized her, silencing her tongue even as her mind screamed. She knew, if she didn't lower the flintlock quickly, his fury would flare.

She'd deceived herself, thinking him gone long enough that his absence might be forever.

"Stop gaping at me, woman." Dropping his weapon by the riverbank, he took a swaggering step toward her. "A wife should strip off her clothes when her husband returns from trapping."

The stench of alcohol preceded him, as if it coated his ropy forearms and sank into the stains of his fringed deerskin shirt. Bile washed up her throat. She blinked once, hoping this was just a nightmare. He'd been gone nearly eighteen months. She had determined—if he ever returned—never again to placate him, or speak softly, or do what he bade in order to survive.

Never again.

The flintlock lay heavy in her grip, but she steadied her aim.

He laughed. "Still think you're too good for the likes of me, woman?" He jerked his chin to the woods beyond. "Go ahead. Run. You know I like a good chase."

Her finger sought the trigger and she realized with a dip of her stomach that she hadn't yet primed the flashpan with black powder.

Quick—she had to be quick.

Seizing the powder horn at her waist, she uncorked it with her teeth. By the time she tipped the mouth over the flashpan, Eduard had closed the distance between them, seized the barrel of the flintlock, tore it out of her hands, and threw a clenched fist that hit her square in the jaw.

Light exploded behind her eyes. She twisted as she fell, the ground jarring her hands and wrists. Her mouth filled with dirt. Dry pine needles pierced her arms. She spit out blood and watched it soak into mud.

A bark of a laugh exploded above her. "There's the position a wife *should* be in when her husband comes home after a long journey."

Ice shot through her, her skin chilled as if with a rime of frost. She dug her elbows into the dirt and struggled to scuttle away, but Eduard yanked her still by the ankles, before throwing wide her legs.

Stinking of bear grease, he pinned her down, grunting and cackling as he tossed up her skirts. Air bathed her backside, which he slapped. Fighting him would be futile, and screaming useless. A husband could do what he wished with his wife—no outsider would intervene.

She wouldn't dare make any noise anyway, for the person most likely to hear her scream would be Etienne. She'd bite through her own lip before summoning him to witness another degradation.

She curled her fingers into the dirt, bracing herself for what was to come. She heard him fumbling with his leather belt. She told herself, *I'm not really here.* She mentally put herself in the window seat at the Salpêtrière Orphanage, reading Virgil by the light of the sun pouring through mullioned windows.

A blood-curdling shout cut through the wilderness, an echo to the unbroken scream in her head. She inhaled so sharply she sucked in a spray of dirt before coughing and spitting it out. Before the warrior cry ended, she heard a tremendous *crack*.

Eduard grunted, and then a great weight pinned her legs. She yanked her limbs from under his weight, shoving her skirts down as she twisted to see what had happened.

Her fiend of a husband lay across the ground, clutching the bloody back of his head. Over him stood Etienne, wielding a flintlock by the bore, the butt of the weapon dripping blood.

Oh, my poor boy.

He'd learned that war cry from the Montagnais chief who had camped nearby, a fatherly presence for Etienne that she'd welcomed in her husband's absence. Her son had never launched that cry with such feeling. Now he stood heaving, the growing man in him come to the fore for the first time in her eyes.

"Why did you come back?" Etienne shouted over his prone father in a voice that didn't crack. "No one wants you here."

Eduard rolled over, clutching the back of his head. "You strike your own father, boy?"

"You're no father to me." Etienne raised the butt of the gun, threatening. "I'm not your son."

She whispered Etienne's name.

He looked at her, eyes wide, his fingers flexing over the flintlock. "I won't let him hurt you anymore, Mother. I'm going to kill him this time."

"No." She struggled to a sitting position. "Don't do it. Don't become like him."

How many times had she stepped between young Etienne and his father's cruelty? She'd always feared that growing up in a house of hate would twist her son's spirit, harden his heart. Now, witnessing Etienne's untamed fury made her ache to the bone. Yes, maybe Eduard deserved to die. But if Etienne were to kill his father, the boy's soul would harden in ways she couldn't heal.

Etienne grunted as Eduard launched a savage kick. Her boy buckled to his knees.

Ignoring a sharp pain in her wrist, she pushed herself up and lunged at Eduard. He shoved her away with enough force to send her sprawling. Scrabbling up against dizziness, she saw the two figures, alike except in height and coloring, facing each other in a crouch.

"The cub's got claws." A sneer curled Eduard's lips as he raised his dirty fists. "Let's see if he knows how to use them."

No, no, don't let him bait you.

But Etienne lunged. Father and son toppled to the ground. Man and boy rolled, grappling, fists flying, toward the riverbank.

Panicked, she looked around for any weapon—a rock, a sturdy stick—and caught sight of her own flintlock on the ground where Eduard had flung it.

She swept it up, noting it was already loaded but still not primed. She seized her powder horn and tapped the mouth against the flintlock pan until black powder spilled. No time to wipe it clean—Etienne grunted, and his mouth leaked blood.

She hefted her weapon, cocked it, and set the butt against the hollow of her shoulder.

"Hell, you're nothing but a button buck, boy." Eduard, sitting astride the boy, delivered a vicious blow and then shoved his face close to Etienne's. "When you pull a gun on a man, you'd better squeeze the trigger."

The weight of the situation fell upon her like a slung fisherman's net. She aimed for Eduard's greasy head, but it was inches away from Etienne's own. She could aim for the gut, but even if she hit him there, Eduard wouldn't go down fast. He'd have time to seize his own weapon and kill them both before she could clumsily reload. No, the pellets in her flintlock had to pierce his head or his heart.

She aimed as if under the judgment of angels.

The birds stopped singing. Wind paused in the trees. The gun weighed a thousand pounds.

She tried to take a step closer to the target, but her feet went leaden. She watched as her husband stretched to retrieve his own discarded flintlock.

Etienne took advantage of the shift in Eduard's weight to scrabble back on his elbows. He threw out a hand to seize his own weapon, lying close. A *loaded* weapon.

She didn't doubt that Etienne, while screaming a war-whoop, had primed his flintlock at a full-tilt run as he'd been taught, her wonderful boy born of this wilderness.

All at once, her husband shot to his feet. Both man and boy raised their weapons.

In the span of a second, she realized this was no longer rough-housing, if it ever had been. Eduard would not shoot wide—and neither would Etienne. Her sight sharpened, finger tightening on the trigger with new urgency. She would not permit Etienne to kill his own father. Better to bear the blood guilt herself, even if she were to be hanged for it.

The flintlock boomed, shoved her back, and sent birds scattering from the trees.

CHAPTER TWENTY-THREE

The confession done, Cecile pressed against Theo's shoulder, head bowed, listening to his heart pounding under her ear like Huron war drums. She felt deflated, as if the whole terrible story had unloaded into the silence like a tipped cart of fieldstone. She remained curled up against him, terrified at what she might see if she dared to peel her cheek off his chest and look up into eyes that only moments ago had been filled with desire and adoration.

"Ceci." His voice rumbled. "You saved your son. It had to be done."

She let go of the breath she hadn't realized she'd been holding. Hadn't she told herself the same thing—*it had to be done*—a thousand times? Yet no matter how many times she repeated those words, they'd never burrowed deep enough to take root.

"Theo…" She gasped. "You believe me?"

"Every word."

"But—"

"No exceptions." He made a growling sound as he reached down to touch the burn scars at her hip and then reached up to trace the scar by her hairline. "I see what he's done to you. Had you told me you'd planned a cold-blooded execution, I would still say you did what had to be done."

His acceptance unstitched her, but she wasn't sure she was ready to forgive herself. "Theo, I still took a life."

"If you hadn't had that flintlock in hand, you would have flung yourself between those two. Am I right? You would have taken the bullet yourself."

She would have. No question. But that wouldn't have stopped Eduard, and Etienne still would have been in danger. She squeezed her eyes shut to fight a tornado of emotions.

"This is why you wanted to join the convent." He gave her a nudge as if to loosen her whelk-like body-curl. "You were seeking absolution."

"You think too well of me." Was forgiveness possible for such a mortal sin? "I wanted to join the convent for sanctuary from the law."

He had been running his fingers down her naked back, but now they stilled. "Why would you need sanctuary? Is your husband still—"

"He's gone." She had hit the man full center. She'd seen him fall back into the river and sink. She and Etienne had stood at the river's edge, breathing hard and in a state of numb shock. "He won't be back."

"Witnesses?"

"None but birds. And Etienne."

"Good."

"There's…another complication." She braced herself. "Talon has begun an investigation into my husband's absence. There's no stopping it. I won't legally be a widow until Talon declares me so."

"Then the investigation must proceed." He pressed his lips against the top of her head and then slid down so they were face-to-face. He cupped one cheek. "After so much time, and no witnesses, the law won't find you."

She lost herself in his kind, loving eyes, wanting to believe he was right. Wanting to believe he wasn't just telling her what she wanted to hear. Wanting to believe that dreams really could come true.

With that impetus, she leaned in and kissed him, letting hope rise along with a thousand other sensations. Skimming her palm across his chest, she nudged herself closer to his strong, beautiful body. How well they moved against each other, yielding and bending and pressing close.

When he slid atop her and entered her with a groan of his own, he knit their fingers together and pushed her arms above her head. He kissed her and moved with her and kissed her again until pleasure consumed them both.

After, as she drifted down from the peak of her excitement, she became aware of the fur blanket lifting, the cold air tingling her skin as he wiped her belly clean. His lips fell like a spark between her breasts before he covered them both up again.

"My Ceci." His green eyes lit with a brightness that wasn't just from the reflected glow of the stove's golden-red coals. "I am in awe of the woman who came to me tonight, sharing so much more than her body."

"I am yours." The truth didn't frighten her anymore. "Now and forever."

"In that case…" He pressed his forehead against hers. "Let's get married."

The next morning, Theo stepped out of the barn into the bite of the morning chill, but nothing could dampen the warmth flooding through him. Cecile had left the barn earlier, for the sake of appearances, to slip back to the cabin in the pre-dawn. She had promised not to say a word about their engagement—even to Marie—until Theo joined them for breakfast.

Breakfast couldn't come soon enough.

Following her wind-faded footprints through a dusty covering of snow, he swiped some firewood from the pile by the side of the cabin. Stepping onto the porch, he pulled the door open just like every other morning, except this time he fought down a grin. He called out a hearty greeting as his gaze passed across the warm room to Marie, sitting with her back to everyone, nursing, then to Lucas at the table, finishing a bowl of sagamité, and then straight to Cecile where his gaze stopped. She was bending over a steaming pot by the hearth fire, her hair damp at her temples, her cheeks flushed from steam, fighting her own smile.

"There you are." Captain Girard slammed a meaty hand on the table, making everyone jump. "Lazing about past dawn, are we?"

Theo stilled. The captain's silver gaze narrowed pinpoint fierce, and the tone of his voice ran rough. The captain usually greeted him in a more jovial way. A side glance at Cecile suggested she was just as surprised at the captain as he.

"Here I thought you'd be up at first light." Lucas clanked his pewter spoon beside his bowl. "Are you so eager to leave us for Quebec—and a berth on a ship to France?"

Was *that* the trouble? The captain hadn't been happy, yesterday, when Theo had informed him of his decision to leave. But the burly Lucas hadn't reacted with nearly as much passion as now. "Actually," Theo ventured, crouching by the hearth to set the firewood in the bin. "I've been thinking—"

"Oh," Lucas interrupted, "you've been *thinking*, have you?"

"Lucas." The warning came from Marie, still nursing the baby on the far side of the room.

"You're only *thinking*," the captain continued, "about the ship you'll be sailing out of these settlements. That's the only thing on your mind, Theo Martin, now that you're finally a free man."

Free man echoed in his head.

He swayed on his heels. He'd been counting down the days to freedom for four long years. How could he have overlooked—even for a moment when he'd arisen from his bed this morning—that his indentured servitude had finally come to an end?

"Congratulations, Theo."

The sight of Cecile answered his own question. He'd forgotten because this woman filled his mind now. This woman who, once all the complications were settled, would be this free man's wife.

"So," Lucas prompted, still frowning, "was it the packing of the canoe that made you late to the table? Or is it that you can't wait to be gone?"

"There will be no berth on a ship for me." Theo swelled with pride and wonder, unsteady in this new freedom. "I'll be staying in these settlements."

"Why?" Lucas barked. "Did the Saint Lawrence River ice up early, making travel impossible? Or do you think you've missed the last ship?"

Theo glanced at Cecile, silently questioning whether this was the time to announce their news. She remained stunned—and mum—watching the captain while holding the wooden spoon suspended above the pot.

Theo stalled. "I've got my reasons for staying, Captain. Good reasons."

"What a man of whims you've turned out to be." Pewter utensils and earthenware bowls rattled as the captain slammed both hands against the table again. "Only yesterday, you were so eager to go. Damn it, man—"

"Lucas, language." Marie glanced over her shoulder toward the hearth, where the two-year-old Charles sat on a braided rug, eyes wide above the wooden toy he was gumming.

The captain grunted, but he did not cease his glower. "So, then, are you just to stay in the settlements until the spring ships come and then leave us?" He pointed at Cecile. "Are you going to break that woman's heart?"

Realization struck Theo hard. *Ah, so that's the root of this matter.* The captain knew he and Cecile had spent the night together.

"Enough." Cecile stepped toward Lucas, holding the dripping wooden spoon aloft. "Captain, I know you're standing in the place where my father would, if I'd ever known my father, but I won't have you roaring at this good man."

"Good man, you say? Are you daft, woman—"

"Careful." Theo took a step toward the table. "No one talks like that to my future wife."

The room went stone silent but for the slobbering sounds of little Charles sucking on the toy.

Damn, had he really said that aloud? He and Cecile were supposed to announce this together. He turned to her with an apology on his face, only to find her grinning.

"I suppose it was foolish," Cecile said, "to think we could keep this from them for more than a moment."

"Keep it from us?" Marie stood from the chair, the nursing done, her bodice-scarf tucked in. Patting the babe against her shoulder, she headed toward the cradle beside the hearth, tsking every step of the way. "As if we couldn't figure it out for ourselves."

"I told you, *Chepewéssin*," the captain said, using Marie's Huron nickname. "I won't believe it until I hear it out of this blackguard's mouth." The captain shot to his full height. "And now that it's been said, it's the *finest* of news, Theo. The *finest*."

Lucas bellowed a laugh, a roar that rattled the pewterware anew, before thrusting a hand toward him.

Theo extended his own, wincing at the grip.

"I promise you," Lucas said, shaking Theo's hand as if he were trying to set it loose from his wrist, "if you had tried to take a canoe and leave this girl behind, I'd have sent you off in bruises."

A warning as well as a congratulations, Theo thought, and both enthusiastically spoken.

Lucas came around the table, seized him by the shoulders, and gifted him with a bone-rattling shake.

Marie, having put the baby in the cradle, approached to embrace Cecile. Both women spoke at the same time in high, merging voices. The excitement in the room was palpable even to little Charles, who pushed to his feet and hurled himself at his father's calf. The captain released Theo only to sweep the toddler up into his arms.

"We heard Ceci sneak off last night," Lucas said, a grin taking the place of outrage. "Those porch floorboards—I haven't fixed them on purpose. I know if someone's coming—or going." He winked. "If my wife hadn't held me back, I'd have come roaring out of bed, rolled up my sleeves—"

"'Mind your own affairs,' I said," Marie interrupted. "I knew the two of them would figure things out, if they ever got a moment alone."

Cecile looked abashed, standing with Marie's hands tight on her shoulders. She sucked her bottom lip between her teeth in a way that made Theo's pulse leap.

"So, you're staying here for the winter, then." Lucas hugged the toddler in one arm as he smacked Theo on the shoulder with his free hand. "Good. I can always use a strong hand to keep the woodpile stocked, clear a path to the smokeroom, and hunt some elk. Cecile can help Marie with the children. And come spring, we'll figure out Cecile's pesky widowhood issue, get you two married, and you'll build me a stone church."

Gratitude rushed through Theo faster than he could think.

"Since nobody is leaving today," Marie announced, "I'll serve breakfast. Lucas, you can feed Charles."

Lucas sat on the creaking chair and settled the toddler on his lap. Marie took the wooden spoon from Cecile's hand and bustled back to the pot. Cecile slipped to the table, slid into her seat, and patted the seat of the chair beside hers until Theo rustled up enough sense to lower himself into it.

"There's plenty more of this." Marie placed in front of him and his future wife two bowls of steaming sagamité, scattered with dried blueberries and a swirl of maple syrup. "Eat your fill. New lovers need sustenance."

Cecile choked on her first bite.

"Oh, Ceci, we're all adults here." Marie's gaze slid to her son. "Except for Charles, who is too young to understand. So, no shame in asking for a second serving to keep up your stamina. Lucas and I understand."

Theo caught the silent communication that passed between his hosts. The air throbbed like a heartbeat. When he looked at Cecile, it throbbed again.

"One more thing." The captain filled a spoon and lifted it to Charles, who leaned forward, mouth opening. "I've been saving a fine plot of land just west of here for someone Marie approves of. I'm always looking for good tenants, and you've proven to be a hardworking man. Now that you're free, if you're willing to throw up a cabin and work the land, I'd be much obliged."

"It's walking distance from here." Marie settled in the fourth chair with her own bowl. "What do you think?"

Theo was still trying to absorb Lucas's offer to stay for the winter. And now, the captain offered housing and land.

He spoke the only truth he could muster. "I don't know what to say—"

"Fortunately, I do." Cecile slipped her hand over his. "Theo and I are grateful for the offer, Captain, but we haven't had time to discuss many things, including the future."

"Haven't had time?" Marie raised a brow. "And here I thought you spent an entire night—"

"Wife." Lucas nudged her shoulder, then returned his attention to wiping sagamité off his son's chin. "There's no rush. You two have the entire winter to decide your future."

"And," Marie added, with a softer look for the both of them, "we'll be very glad for your company."

Theo patted his heart in silent thanks, then turned his attention to the porridge. As the tartness of a blueberry burst on his tongue, he realized how hungry he was. He took another spoonful, and yet another, the sweet flavor of maple filling his mouth. Sagamité had never tasted so good—yet it was the same recipe as every morning. Even back in Guéret his breakfast had often been a wheat porridge, nothing unusual.

Still grappling with the swift change of events, he shook his head and then opened his eyes in a way that went beyond just lifting his lids.

In one deep sweep of the room, he took in the golden glow and the people within it, chattering away with ease. He saw how the captain made a face at his son, prompting a toddler's laugh like the ringing of chimes. A crackling hearth fire warmed them all, and the light played among the strands of Cecile's blonde hair.

The sight melded with a dream of a future he hadn't planned for, but that now lay promised before him like a sky full of stars.

"Do you hear that?" Lucas straightened to glance at the oilskin-covered window, while his son on his lap lunged toward the spoon held suspended before him. "Marie, are we expecting visitors?"

"Maybe it's Hateya, coming to check on me again."

The captain shook his head and so did Theo— for he heard more than one body shuffling through the new powdered snow in the clearing outside. A family of deer, perhaps, cavorting into the clearing to scrape for grass? Venison would make a hearty dinner.

Lucas must have had the same thought, for he handed the toddler to Marie before standing to grab his flintlock. Theo pushed up from his chair to follow.

"Saints Almighty," Lucas muttered as he swung open the door and stepped outside. "What are *you* rascals doing here?"

Theo came around the captain but saw no deer or elk. What he did see were three soldiers in bright blue uniforms, their canoe pulled up at the riverbank.

"Forgive the intrusion, Captain Girard." The front soldier saluted sheepishly. "I know it's early, but I've been ordered here on official business."

"Lieutenant," Lucas began with a sigh, "I've told your colonel more than once that I'm married with children now and have no interest in returning to service. Stubborn goat, he is—"

"It's not about that, sir." The lieutenant fished a paper out from between the brass buttons of his coat. "I have orders to arrest a Madame Cecile Tremblay."

CHAPTER TWENTY-FOUR

Shivering on the hay-strewn floor of her jail cell, Cecile hugged her knees to her chest. Three days of nothing but bread and water had left the walls of her stomach scraping together. Rocking for warmth, she yearned for sunlight, a wool cloak, and uninterrupted sleep. And yet, in a strange way, she was grateful that thoughts of worldly needs consumed her, for they turned her mind away from the phantom rope tightening around her neck.

A clank of an iron key jerked her alert. She glanced beyond the bars of her cell to the rattling wooden door of the shed. Was it time for another interrogation?

The door swung open, and light poured in, slinging daggers into her eyes.

"Terce bells will be ringing soon," said one of her guards, speaking to someone following him in through the blinding light. "At the first chime, your time is up. Got it?"

A man grunted an assent—deep-chested, rumbling—and at the sound Cecile's heart leapt. Scrambling to her feet, she pushed filthy fingers down her unkempt braid. The closing of the door engulfed the shed in darkness again. Gripping the iron bars that kept her caged in a corner, the sole prisoner in the room, she blinked as Theo's figure approached through hazy filaments of light seeping through the badly caulked walls.

With a half sob, she shot an arm through the bars to touch him, fingers grazing his jaw. He sported an inflamed cut on his brow and a black eye from the beating he'd taken for trying to save her from the arresting soldiers.

"Oh, Theo." She hazarded a gasp, her throat dry. "Does it hurt?"

"It's nothing." He slid his hands between the bars, hissing as his warm hands cupped her cheeks. "You're *freezing.*"

He released her long enough to shrug off his cloak and shove the garment between the bars. As he struggled to settle it across her shoulders, the wool cocooned her in pine-fragrant warmth.

With Theo's battered face only inches away, she noted another scratch on his throat and a split in the lobe of his right ear, healed over in the three days they'd been apart, but still red and angry.

She ran a finger over a nick on his short-whiskered jaw. "What have they done to you, my love?"

"You're the one suffering." He tugged the collar so the cloak would cover her more fully. "And you're worried about my bruises."

"I thought..." She swallowed hard. On the day she'd been arrested, the last thing she'd seen, as one guard had pushed her toward the canoe, had been Theo grappling with the two other soldiers blocking his way. "Those soldiers' flintlocks were primed, Theo... I thought—"

"The captain pulled us apart before any real blood was spilled." He huffed in frustration. "I don't think any other man but Lucas could have managed that."

"It was foolish of you to fight." She slid her hands through the bars to grip the linen of his shirt, to feel the warmth of him in the fibers. "You might have been arrested—"

"They tried. But the captain knew the soldiers and talked them out of it." He ran his thumbs over her cheeks. She couldn't tell whether the roughness was due to the calluses on his hands or the gritty soil on her face. "That doesn't matter. I'm safe, Lucas is safe, Marie is safe. You are *not*. I've been trying to see you for days."

He pressed his face against the bars, gripped her cheeks in place, and locked his lips over hers.

A gasp died in her throat. His strength flooded through her, melted her spine, urged her to lean into him as far as she could despite the iron bars between them. She couldn't quite feel her feet upon the hay anymore—she might as well be levitating.

He murmured her name as he tilted his head, shooting his fingers into her loosened, plaited hair, squeezing with desperation, speaking words she no longer understood as language, but only as the melody of love.

He finally pulled away, pressing his forehead against hers as best he could with iron bars keeping them apart. She'd thought she had no more tears to shed, but they prickled, now, at the backs of her eyes. Tears not of sorrow or fear but of a swelling love for this beautiful man.

What a tragedy, that such a love arrived in her life only when her life was soon to end.

He cleared his throat and pulled back from the bars, taking in the small shed and the smaller cage, glaring at the narrowness of her cell and then at the empty pewter plate on the floor next to a dry, tipped-over cup.

"We don't have much time," he said. "Have they interrogated you yet?"

"Yes. On the first day and yesterday, and I suspect they'll be back today." She swallowed, her throat sore. "They take me out of this cage, put irons on my wrists and ankles—"

Theo grunted and seized her hands, raising them for his perusal. The grunt deepened as he turned them over and saw the chafed marks on her wrists.

"Who," he asked, fury rippling through his words, "did this?"

"Soldiers—different ones. They change my guards every day."

"Did they hurt you in any other way?"

A fresh chill washed over her. "Not…not yet."

Theo nodded, but she knew by the sudden stoniness of his face that he, too, was banking panic.

"The interrogators," he continued, placing her hands palm to palm so he could cover them both with his own, warmer ones. "What are their names?"

"They didn't say, but I can describe them." She shivered at the memory as she described the trio of interrogators to Theo, down to their velvet coats and lace collars, each man colder-eyed than the next. "I suspect they are the investigators sent by Talon, but I can't be sure."

"Seems likely." He met her gaze, his green one deadly serious. "What evidence do they have?"

"I don't know." She caught a sob before she became undone. "They asked me the same questions in a hundred different ways, but they tell me nothing. Except that they found his…body."

"Yes, I heard that in the tavern." Theo released her hands and slid his arms through the bars to wrap them around her so he could draw her close enough to whisper in her ear. "They found him on a bank of an island at the mouth of a river out of Trois-Rivières."

Her mind screamed. He tightened his grip as if he heard her distress. She squeezed her eyes shut. To think she'd once been considered the good girl. The orphan all the nuns had adored. The one student who'd never felt the smack of a ruler on her hand. The woman who would never throw herself into danger like Marie or flaunt disobedience like Genny, yet had done something a thousand times grimmer, bloodier, more unforgivable.

"The river," Theo whispered, as his gaze darted to the shed walls that were riddled with cracks and lingering shadows. "It runs by most of the homes in Trois-Rivières. Homes owned by those who might not have liked Eduard Tremblay either. According to gossip, your husband was deeply in debt to a lot of people. Do you have any idea why Talon's investigators would single you out?"

Because I'm guilty.

"Whatever they found," he said, thinking aloud, "it can't be enough to convict you. That's why you're still being interrogated. They need a confession."

Icy fingers squeezed her mute. She knew that if the authorities failed to get a confession by questioning her, they would use more violent tactics. They might pound wedges beneath the wooden staves of a boot. Lay a braided whip against her back. Or brand her in places unseen.

"Ceci." Theo pulled back to meet her eyes. "You didn't sign any papers, did you?"

"No." Though the interrogators were wearing her down. She'd become keenly aware that telling the truth of what happened would put an end to the exhaustion, the hunger, and the whole investigation. All her worries would end—but so would her life.

"Lie," he whispered with force. "Lie over and over again and never sign anything."

A tear slipped down her cheek. She plunged into his gaze, steady with determination. Darling Theo, so worried for her…but she had been doomed from the start. Perhaps, from the very moment Eduard had returned to raise a fist to Etienne, she had known she would end up with a rope around her neck. She'd been flailing ever since, trying to stave off the inevitable, holding desperately to the faintest thread of hope.

And now here she was, dragging Theo into her nightmare.

She sank a little in his arms. She was so tired of fighting. She didn't regret fighting Eduard. She didn't regret preventing herself and Etienne from being slaughtered like lambs, but she *did* kill a man. Furthermore, her actions had put everyone she loved in terrible danger. If she confessed, the torment would be over.

And she'd be protecting everyone else, too.

Straightening, she pulled herself away from the iron bars and the man beyond them, urging him to let his arms fall away.

"You're a free man, Theo." What a beautiful name he had. What a life they could have built together on the wooded banks of the Saint Lawrence River. "You can go and do whatever you want now. Forget about me."

His eyes blazed like green fire. "I will never leave you."

"I release you from all promises." Her throat closed, as if already encircled by a prickly hemp rope. "The magistrates will hang me, no matter what—"

"They have no evidence." He gripped the bars. "They can't convict you if you don't confess."

"They convicted you four years ago, and you didn't confess."

"That situation was different. The viscount paid for false witnesses." He rattled the bars. "If I have to put my own head in the noose, Ceci, I will see you freed."

"That's the problem." She fixed this moment in her memory—the chill of the air, the fierceness of his expression, the love on his face. This would be the remembrance she would fill her mind with when she climbed the scaffold. "If you do anything rash, they'll arrest you, too."

"Ceci—"

"I'm not saying I'll confess." She wasn't sure she could bear this discussion much longer. "I do value my life…but I'm not as strong as you think I am." She raised a hand. "Please, let's not argue. Let's talk of other things. Tell me about Etienne."

Theo frowned at the change in topic, concern still writ large upon his face. "He is safe. Sister Martha broke the rules to keep him inside the convent."

"Did soldiers come for him, too?"

"For interrogation, yes. But the Reverend Mother refused to let the soldiers into the convent, or bring Etienne out to them."

Her relieved sigh emptied her lungs to the dregs.

"You should have seen her, Ceci." Theo's chest rose and fell, the line between his brows narrowing. "Sister Martha fought like a general. She never denied that Etienne was inside the schoolhouse. He was shouting, everyone could hear him. 'He's but a child,' she told the soldiers. 'A child terrified for his mother.' She warned the soldiers that they'd have to knock her down, breach the sanctuary of a holy house, and be accountable to the bishop himself if they dared to take the boy by force."

She gripped a bar to stay upright. She owed Sister Martha a thousand Hail Marys and a million Our Fathers.

Etienne has sanctuary.

At least one of Cecile's foolish plans had won out. "Did you speak with my son?"

"Not yet. Sister Martha had to lock him in a closet to keep him from coming to the fort in a rage.

That's what the screaming was about. He's furious at your arrest."

"Promise me you'll protect him." Outside, the sonorous chime of the first terce bell rang from the fort's chapel, signaling their time was up. "Most importantly, keep him away from the court, and the investigators, and the law."

"You don't want him to testify."

"Of course not. Self-defense is no defense at all in this situation. We both know that. Also… there's another matter. A secret I still haven't told you."

Theo's face darkened. "Tell me. I need to know everything."

She breathed in deep, gathering courage to say what must be said so that Theo could protect Etienne long after she was gone.

"Two weapons were fired that terrible day, Theo. Only one of them was mine." She swallowed a lump speared with a thousand sharp pins. "But I have sworn—on all the angels and saints—that I will be the only one to hang for this crime."

Though the sun shone brightly overhead, Theo trudged back to the convent lost in a mental fog, parsing out what a shivering, exhausted, too-thin Cecile had just confessed from her jail cell. He should have recognized the truth earlier. Now he understood why she'd been so stubbornly determined to find Etienne a seat in a monastery school, though the boy had the aptitude, skill, and desire to work with stone. Etienne needed sanctuary that a building site couldn't provide but a monastery school could.

Such was a mother's love.

"Monsieur Martin!"

Theo raised his head to find the Reverend Mother huffing and puffing as she surged full steam across the chapel building site.

He took a few jogging steps to meet her halfway. "What is it?"

"He's gone."

No need to ask who she was talking about. He looked all around him, up and down the road, toward the banks of the Saint Lawrence River and then farther past the road to the edge of the woods and a gristmill. No sign of a slim boy, or flapping fringe, or flowing dark hair.

He said, "How did he get out?"

"I was a fool." She gripped her hips while gasping for breath. "He was crying, the poor thing, when I took him food. We talked as he ate. He asked for some work, said the idleness was driving him mad." She shook her head, the cross hanging from her neck swinging. "I sent him to chop wood just outside—"

"How long ago?"

"No more than a few minutes. I went in to get his coat. He seemed so subdued." She ran a hand over her brow. "When I came out, it was like the Good Lord Himself had snatched him up to the heavens. I saw his footprints in the grass, heading toward this road. That's what I was just following. Heaven save us, where did he go?" The nun glanced beyond Theo, along the road to Montreal, and grasped her cross. "If Etienne went to confront the magistrate—"

"He didn't pass me on the road. He couldn't have gone far."

Theo followed the nun to where she'd seen footprints, then he trailed them to some scuffs across the rutted road. On the opposite verge, Theo discovered a fresh, wet outline of a muddy boot pressed into the frost-glazed grass and farther up the slope.

"Reverend Mother," he said, turning toward her. "Jules is still at the building site, stacking fieldstone. Tell him to head toward the fort, just in case Etienne slipped by us. Tell him he must bring the boy back, even if he has to knock him out and haul him over his shoulder."

The sister nodded and set off to find Jules.

Theo followed the path of the footprints. Some ways up the slope, he passed a matted-down place in a swale of longer grass, where the boy must have burrowed to avoid detection after the nun came out to find him gone.

Theo came upon Etienne around the back of the gristmill, slumped against the mossy wall. Making scuffing noises as he approached, Theo waited for the boy to notice his arrival. Etienne didn't lift his head. Only by the tightening of shoulders did Theo realize the boy was aware that he was no longer alone.

Shifting his gaze toward a fringe of thick woods, Theo leaned against the gristmill wall. He was the wrong person to be talking to Etienne about his mother. Theo had saved the boy's life the first day they met, but gratitude had long been replaced with a sullen hostility. The boy had sensed the growing relationship between Theo and his mother long before either one of them had admitted it.

Considering the violence in the boy's upbringing, Etienne's protectiveness of his mother was something to admire. Now, seeing him slumped in despair. Theo felt as if a lead weight hung on his own heart.

Theo lowered himself to a crouch, the wall of the gristmill at his back.

The boy, chin on his knees, yanked hunks of grass from the ground and tossed them away. The boy's mind seemed to be spinning with the same heaving force as the arms of the windmill above their heads.

A dozen full rotations passed before Etienne ventured a word.

"I am going to testify." He threw a chunk of sod farther away than the others. "My mother can't stop me. Neither can you."

The boy was talking big, but there was no mistaking the iron determination in his words. Theo wondered if it would be better to treat the boy less like a runaway and more like the man he was becoming—the man he would need to be, to survive all of this.

Theo said, "I just spoke to your mother."

His head jerked up. "Is she all right?"

"She's tired. Cold. Worried about you." Theo laid his head back against the wall. His heart squeezed at the memory of Cecile's icy fingers and the violet shadows under her eyes. "She's determined to protect you at all costs."

"She's the one who needs protecting." The boy tossed a tuft of grass and folded his arms around his upraised knees. "She's the one who's going to be hanged."

"She won't hang. I swear it—"

"You can't swear it." A vein throbbed at the boy's temple. "She told me about you, you know. The night before she went to the Girards'. She told me why you're an indentured servant and what happened back in Paris. She said that while she was gone, I needed to *respect* you in all things."

Sounds like her order didn't stick.

"That's why you can't swear she won't hang." Etienne's nostrils flared. "You know my mother won't get a fair trial."

"I'll set her free anyway."

"Impossible. She's in a cage in the fort. There's no escaping a place so well guarded."

"If she's convicted, they will have to take her to Quebec. Worst case, I'll rescue her from the tumbrel."

"And then what?" Etienne turned angry black eyes on him. "You'll both be hunted down."

"The wilderness"—Theo gestured toward the fringe of trees at the height of the slope as he remembered Cecile's own words—"is wide and deep."

"She would hate living in the wilderness. She would hate always running from the law." Etienne turned his face away. "Mom should be living in a palace with servants and lots of food. She should have nothing harder to do than embroider all day."

Those words were a kick in the gut, for Theo wanted to give her exactly all that. But first, she needed her freedom.

"Only I can free her," Etienne insisted. "By going to the magistrate and telling the truth."

Theo swallowed a scoff. "She told you what happened to me, and you still believe the truth will matter here?"

"You don't know what happened that day." Etienne flung his words. "If you did, you'd march me to the magistrate yourself."

"I *do* know everything."

That got a twitch out of the boy—and then a stony stillness, the whir of the windmill blades loud above them.

"Your mother trusts me, Etienne." Having this conversation was like creeping through sand flats with hidden sinkholes. "After everything she's gone through, think of how difficult that must have been. I will not break that trust, not to her and not to you either."

The boy swiveled his head, hiding his face, clearly grappling with the dilemma of whether to trust him or not. Theo waited, sensing nothing he said would make a difference. The boy was turning into a man—he must make his own decision.

"If she told you everything," Etienne said in a low, shaking voice, "then you know it was self-defense. That bastard had nearly killed Mom a hundred times—sometimes sober or, like that day, in a murderous drunk…"

The story tumbled out. Etienne told of how he'd heard her cry out in the woods, how he'd come running, how he'd stepped between them. He'd nearly lost consciousness at the first blow. He'd come to with his father looming over him, spitting hate. He'd crawled back from him, thrown his arms wide, and felt against his palm the bore of his own already-loaded weapon.

He'd raised it only to find himself staring down the bore of his father's weapon.

Two blasts had echoed through the woods.

Etienne finished on a strangled sob. Theo gave the boy a few moments to gather himself.

Only then did Theo speak the same words he'd said to Cecile. "You did what had to be done, Etienne."

Etienne's Adam's apple bobbed.

"If you go to the magistrates and confess what you just told me, they'll call you both guilty." Theo's jaw tightened at the thought. "Have you considered your mother's agony if she had to watch you die on the scaffold beside her?"

"This isn't fair." The boy's lips thinned. "It's not *right.*"

"I agree." Theo pulled a piece of grass from the ground, as the boy had been doing, peeling it apart as he spoke. "Someday, there may come a better system of justice that will be blind to money and power. A system that won't use torture to elicit confessions. One that will take into account the greater circumstances when determining guilt or innocence. Like for the father who steals bread for the sole purpose of feeding his starving family, or the scapegoat convicted of arson because she has no influential friends to help in her defense, or the young man who shoots a violent killer so he—and his mother—won't be murdered in turn. Until that time, Etienne, we have to work with the system that exists."

The boy's chest heaved as he focused on something a thousand miles beyond the crest of the hill. "What you said before, about rescuing her from the tumbrel. Would you…would you really do that?"

"Yes."

The boy shot to his feet and paced away a few steps only to swivel on a heel to stand directly in front of Theo. Etienne looked as prickly and alert as a wary porcupine.

A full-grown one.

"If it comes to that, to rescuing her…" Etienne tilted his chin. "I go with you."

Theo spoke without hesitation. "Agreed."

Ceci wouldn't like the deal, but Theo could tell there'd be no locking Etienne away this time. The boy needed to protect his mother, and Theo would not squash the young man's fiercest and most honorable quality.

Ceci would have to forgive them both later.

And there *would* be a later. For, looking at this young man, an idea had come to Theo—a better, less criminal plan for a chance at a happy future.

"Come with me." Theo slapped a hand on Etienne's shoulder. "Let's set your mother free."

CHAPTER TWENTY-FIVE

Shuffling in chains, Cecile fought to keep her spine straight and her face stony as guards led her across the frozen yard of the Montreal fort to the frontier courthouse. Within those log walls, her future would soon be stripped from her. She held fast to dignity—all she had left.

Passing between the pair of soldiers guarding the door, she squelched a quiver as she stepped into a small antechamber. Holding a quill above the pages of a book, the clerk behind the desk didn't even look up before barking a question.

"Name?"

What foolish officialdom. Was there more than one female prisoner being dragged into court today? The other three cages in the shed had remained empty for the entire week.

With a huff, she said, "Cecile Tremblay."

If only she'd had time to marry Theo before she'd been arrested—and become Cecile Martin. At least then she would have shaken off the last vestige of her husband from her life.

The clerk wrote her name in his book, and then gestured toward a set of double doors. The guards nudged her into a bare-walled courtroom flanked with narrow windows that filled the space with gray light. A long, gleaming table stretched across the back wall. Before it stood rows of chairs at precise intervals. A fenced dais loomed in the center of the room—the box for the accused—and the solders led her between the rows of seats toward it.

Glancing at the dozen or so people already seated, she recognized Montreal's only doctor—also the mortician and coroner—who didn't bother to turn his head to look in her direction.

Then her gaze fell upon a familiar silhouette.

She must have made a sound, for Theo twisted in his chair, swung an arm over the back, and met her gaze with a face that blazed with determination.

He'd come.

He shouldn't have—she should send him a scolding scowl—but her heart surged aloft at the sight of him.

"Step up, miss," a guard prodded as they reached the box.

She did as the soldier commanded, tripping up the step and grasping the rail for balance as she fixed her focus on Theo. He wore new clothes—a blinding-white boiled linen shirt and a fine woolen doublet edged with braid. His breeches bore brass buttons. His hair, pulled back in a neat queue, gave emphasis to the slashes of his cheekbones and the cut of his resolute jaw.

During the days they'd been apart, he'd transformed into a free man of stature. How it warmed her sore heart to know at least one of them had shaken off chains.

"All rise."

At the clerk's announcement, chairs scraped against the wooden floorboards. The tap of a musket barrel urged her to turn her attention forward. A corner door swung open to the magistrates parading in. The judge wore somber black wool. Another man, more finely dressed, followed behind him. His well-oiled wig sported chestnut-colored curls that tumbled to midchest. The gold trim upon his cinched doublet gleamed in the dusky light.

Heavens alive. She clutched the front rail for balance, her wrist shackles ringing. This was the most powerful man in the entire settlement—Intendant Talon himself.

Everyone in the courtroom sat—except for her, for there was no seat in the box. She wasn't sure her knees would bend, anyway, as she'd gone as stiff as a corpse.

Why had Talon come all the way from Quebec on the edge of winter to attend this hearing? Was it for the spectacle, a woman accused of murder? Not to protect a King's Girl, for sure, because when Talon swept up the skirts of his doublet to drop into his seat, he skewered her with a fierce and angry look.

The clerk opened the proceedings by naming her as the accused. He recited the accusation of murder and then called up a witness.

Her shackles clanked. *A witness?*

She glanced at Theo, now casually bracing an elbow on the back of the seat beside him. He didn't flinch at all.

She drew a measure of comfort from his ease. The witness, a man she didn't recognize, tugged on his deerskin tunic and swaggered to the chair. She was too far away to smell him, but she knew such a man would reek of bear-grease. Examining his bearded face and light-colored eyes, she recognized him as a common species of *coureur de bois,* though he was not one of Eduard's old acquaintances.

The lumbering fur trader sat with an arrogant slouch as a clerk approached and raised a sheaf of papers.

Cecile, swaying on her feet, dug half-moons into her palms

"Sir," the clerk said, "I have here your signed testimony that I will now read aloud to this court." The clerk cleared his throat. "On or about the tenth day of June of this year, the deceased, Eduard Tremblay of Trois-Rivières, came out of the wilderness and entered a private drinking house on the westernmost end of the Rue Charles, treating all the card players, including the witness, to wine and brandy paid for by new pelts."

"He could be generous, Eduard could," the man blustered, running his hand down his curly black beard. "That's why I remember—"

"Sir, be so kind as to not interrupt the proceedings." The clerk waved the papers in his hand. "You are here to testify to the truth of your signed statement. You'll have a chance to add detail, but only after I am finished."

Cecile listened to a tale she'd never heard, afraid to breathe. Eduard had returned to Montreal in June with a large haul of furs and gone straight to a gambling den—no surprise there. Much later, he'd bolted up from a losing hand to announce he had a wife hungry for a tumble in Trois-Rivières. At the crudeness of the report, Cecile choked down a wave of nausea.

"And that was the last time this witness saw Eduard Tremblay alive." The clerk lowered the paper. "Is this your true and faithful testimony, sir?"

"It is." The witness tugged on his beard. "Rightly told."

"Is there anything you'd like to add?"

When the witness shrugged, the clerk turned to her in the box.

"Madame Tremblay, it is your prerogative at this time to ask any questions of this witness, to corroborate or to deny his testimony."

A thousand words rose to her lips. Eduard did like gambling. And wine. And brandy. And preferred to spend his coin on his friends rather than on his family. But confirming Eduard's sordid character wouldn't absolve her from the accusation of murder. She could tell that the witness's testimony had already polluted the air with wariness and contempt for her. She would make matters worse if she spoke ill of the dead, so she hesitated. What could she ask? She'd had no warning that there would be witnesses and no idea that she'd be allowed to speak. She dared not look at Theo and get him involved.

In the end, simple truth won out. "I do not know this man, sir." Cecile lowered her chin. "I cannot refute anything he has said."

The clerk shrugged, then flipped through another parchment in his possession. Calling up another rough-looking woods runner, the clerk began reading a similar testimony.

Then the door to the courtroom burst open.

Feet pounded on the courtroom floorboards.

Cecile swung around to witness a crowd of women pouring into the room like a phalanx of skirted soldiers—led by Sister Martha.

The nun winked at her—*winked*—as she charged full sail past the box for the accused to head toward the front table. The nun came to a stop directly in front of the judge and Talon, who'd shoved their seats back as if expecting the women to lunge.

"This proceeding is an *outrage.*" Sister Martha planted her fists on her hips. "And to see you here, Intendant Talon, taking part in this farce."

"What is the meaning of this?" The judge caught hold of himself and arranged his features into a stern expression. "I order you and this rabble to leave—"

"Leave, you say?" Sister Martha's voice quivered with astonishment. "But I've come to testify. The law may weigh the testimony of a woman as worth a fraction of that of a man"—the nun glared back at the rogues' gallery of witnesses now shrinking in their seats—"but, if Madame Tremblay's lessons in mathematics are correct, many fractions add up to a whole. Thus, I've brought with me others who will confirm my testimony to the gentle, spotless character of our much-aggrieved sister in all but blood, Cecile Tremblay, who is *falsely accused.*"

The women crowding the narrow aisle raised their voices in agreement.

Cecile caught her breath at the tumult. Every nun in the congregation was present. As was Marie—darling Marie! —now beaming encouragement, Lucas standing tall at her side.

And— could it be? —there was Marietta, all the way from Quebec, with her husband, Philippe.

And— who was that? —no, it couldn't possibly be.

Cecile blinked at the sight of a tiny redhead in buckskins and leggings decorated with painted porcupine quills. Cecile shook her head, trying to erase the illusion, for her friend Genny couldn't be *here*. Yet the girl-who-couldn't-be-Genny grinned at her, nodding in encouragement.

Cecile choked on a cough. The edge of the railing bit into her hip.

All of these women. All of these friends.

They'd come to save her.

Up front, Sister Martha spoke ever louder to the men ranged behind the table. "Why have you all ignored the complaints I've lodged with your clerk since you sent *soldiers* to fetch a woman who belongs in *my congregation* on charges that defy all reason?"

"This is a court of law," the judge barked. "A murder has been committed, madame—"

"Not by this woman." The nun slung a finger in her direction. "Madame Tremblay couldn't kill a chicken for the pot."

"If the lady is innocent," the judge argued, with an emphasis on *if*, "she will be set free this very day."

"This very *hour*, she will be released." For a short woman, Sister Martha could swell herself up to what seemed like twice her size. "If not, I promise you I shall have a word with the bishop about the government's interference in a place where the church rules."

The women raised their voices to the rafters.

Cecile pressed her hand against her chest to keep her heart from beating out of it. With such forces aligned in her favor, was there a chance for freedom?

Talon rose to his feet, casting his words across the room like oil upon roiling waters. "Madame Tremblay is not your novice yet, Most Reverend Mother. Or has the situation changed since our last correspondence?"

"The situation *will* change," the nun warned, "if this lady isn't freed into my care."

The judge banged his palm on the desk. "She is on trial for a serious matter, and I will not allow such disruption in my courtroom." He waved his reddened hand toward his clerk. "Read the charges." A fresh chorus of garbled voices drowned out the clerk, so the judge raised his voice to booming. "Soldiers, come clear this mob."

"No." Talon gripped the judge's shoulder. "No need of that."

A few soldiers rushed in from the foyer, weapons clanking, but they stopped in their tracks at Talon's sharp shake of his head.

"A word, Sister Martha." Talon seized the cane balanced against his seat. "In the judge's chambers, if you please."

Talon strode to the corner door, cane clicking sharply on the floorboards with every swing. The nun followed.

Cecile startled as a hand gripped her by the elbow. There was Theo, beside the box, his green eyes dancing.

"Come." Theo glared at one soldier, then the other, until both stepped back. "Let's join them."

"How…" she whispered, stumbling along. "How…"

"You are well-loved, Ceci." He bent to speak into her ear as they walked. "More than you know."

They stepped into the judge's low-ceilinged chambers. Talon, who'd slipped a hip onto a desk in the corner, skewered her with that fierce gaze again. Her feet dragged but Theo led her to stand next to Sister Martha, now facing Talon from the middle of the room.

"You've made your point, Reverend Mother." Talon focused sharply on the nun. "I hear your objections. But the process has begun and thus must continue, despite this mob."

Cecile heard the muffled shuffle of small booted feet as others poured into the chamber to join them.

"Monsieur Talon, I would advise you to be prudent." Sister Martha spread her hands. "You are in Montreal, not Quebec. The people here are less constrained by procedure and more motivated by truth."

Talon's face darkened. "Disrespecting authority is a dangerous tactic."

"So is disrespecting the law," came a voice from the back.

Talon lifted his chin toward the source. "Captain Girard. Are you slandering the court?"

"Not the court." Lucas huffed like a bear. "The investigators."

"Be very careful, sir." Talon shifted off the desk. "Those are my investigators you slander."

"Have your investigators spoken to the dozens of men to whom the victim owed a great deal of money?" The captain pulled a sheaf of papers from his waistcoat. "I certainly have, but none of these men are in court today. Not as witnesses, and not charged with Tremblay's murder."

Marietta, dark curls bouncing, stepped forward. "Let that innocent girl go," she said, flinging a hand toward Cecile. "Be done with this nonsense."

"If the law were only so simple, Madame Martineau." Talon's gaze slid from her to her well-dressed husband. "You should constrain your wife, sir."

"Careful, Talon." Phillipe nudged his cloak off his shoulder, the sword at his side gleaming. "Etta speaks the truth. Cecile lived at our house and took care of our children. The wrong person has been accused."

"My, my." Talon shifted his gaze and Cecile felt it like the butt of a rifle in her gut. "How stalwart are your friends, and how eclectic a group. Some are monied and influential." He nodded toward Philippe and Lucas. "And others should be in jail themselves."

Cecile cast a panicked glance toward Genny, standing with one leg cocked like a peacock amid a gaggle of gray-clad nuns. Years ago, Genny had escaped her own trouble with the law by running away with her husband into the wilderness. How reckless for her to be here! Though she appeared nonplussed, one hand flexing over the hilt of a dagger as she met Talon's gaze like a dare.

"Easy, Ceci." Theo's breath brushed against her ear as he stood, stalwart, behind her. "Right now, it's *you* who needs defending."

"We are a varied group," Sister Martha conceded, "but we are united in our conviction of the injustice of these proceedings. So, then, have you seen sense yet, monsieur?"

"Sense." Talon huffed. "Even you, Reverend Mother, must admit there exists a streak of insurrection among a certain group of King's Girls present in these chambers." Talon slammed the tip of his cane on the floor. "You three"—Cecile flinched as Talon pointed at Genny, Marie, and then herself — "have given me more trouble than hundreds of other King's Girls combined."

"Cecile is the best of us," Marie announced in a steady voice. "Do not cast the shadow of our mischief upon her."

"Ah, Madame Girard." Talon straightened. "There's always a price for such mischief. For instance, had you and your accomplices not arrived in a mob—if you, instead, had allowed this process to come to its logical end—you would know by now that I have already reviewed the testimony and found it shamelessly unconvincing."

The breath Cecile sucked in seared a path down her throat.

"I am sure the judge will conclude that the testimony is inconclusive." Talon gathered his fury back into himself, and looked, to Cecile, every inch the king's appointed man. "By normal procedure, Madame Tremblay would then be sent back to interrogation in the hopes of securing a confession–"

"No."

Shouts went up all around. Theo stepped right up to her, warm at her back. She knew, suddenly, that if Talon tried to send her back to that cage, Theo would whisk her out of the courthouse, armed soldiers be damned.

"Let me finish." Talon's voice boomed, and the shouts settled. "I speak for the king, and thus my decision supersedes any procedure. Thus, I make you an offer, Madame Tremblay."

Skewered by the powerful man's glare, Cecile sensed her fate swinging on a fraying string.

"As a King's Daughter, you have certain obligations. Even as a widow. I will give you what this mob wants—a complete acquittal of all charges. But only if you do your duty and marry again."

She had barely absorbed the thrill of the words *a complete acquittal of all charges* before *only if you do your duty and marry again* could register.

Sister Martha turned to her, her mouth making a distressed 'O.'

The offer bounced inside Cecile's skull, making an impact but not in a way she understood.

"I'll marry her."

Theo stepped to her side, standing as straight as a ship's mast as the room went silent.

"This very hour, I'll marry her." He dropped his intense green gaze to her uptilted face. "If she'll consent to honor me with a yes."

CHAPTER TWENTY-SIX

A prisoner in the morning, a bride by evening.

Cecile bolted off the porch of the Girard cabin, sweeping up the skirts of the silk brocade dress Marie had lent her, with its looped overskirt and pretty yellow ribbons. She raced toward Theo, standing amid guests by a cooking fire, wearing the attire of a free man, with brass buttons on his cloak and buttery boots on his feet.

Her footsteps pounded on the grass and her skirts flew in the breeze of her passing, but she couldn't reach him fast enough.

Under a thinning canopy of blazing autumn leaves, the sun spit out just enough gentle warmth to melt a thin layer of snow. She raced past the trestle table set with pewter dishes waiting to be plated with venison now roasting on a spit. Pumpkin fritters cooled in bowls, rustic bread had been thickly sliced, and bottles of wine gleamed in the dappled light.

Such a post-wedding feast, cobbled together by Genny's woodland skill, Marie's swift planning, and Marietta's boundless generosity.

The gathered sisters of the congregation giggled as they witnessed Cecile hurling herself toward her lover.

Sister Martha raised a cup.

Etienne, leaning against the trunk of an oak with the baby porcupine in his arms, laughed even as he lowered his head in mortification.

To think, only hours ago, she had been wearing a wrinkled, dirty dress, her hair tangled, her wrists bearing the marks of shackles, while speaking vows before a priest and witnesses.

Everyone who'd been at the court had joined the wedding—following Talon, who'd purposefully led everyone to the fort chapel himself, to ensure her and Theo's vows were consecrated.

After, everybody had gone to the tavern to toast the marriage. Several of the *coureur de bois* witnesses had graciously stood them a drink. How funny it had been to see the nuns gathered amid a clutch of woods runners and Huron traders, shooting back wine in a smoky public house.

And now, finally, they'd all made their way to the Girard house in a flotilla of woods runners' canoes. With Marie's help, Cecile had changed into better clothes. Now she fought her hampering skirts to run as fast as she could toward *her husband.*

He flung his arms wide as she approached, caught her with a laugh, and swung her in a circle so wide that her dress flew in an arc around them.

She felt his breath against her ear. "My darling Ceci."

Her feet hit the ground but he did not release her.

She touched his jaw, his cheek, the flaring crinkles on either side of his eyes, hardly believing he was real. That *this* was real.

"The first time I saw you, you were racing—just like this—to save Etienne." He tightened his grip. "That's when I fell in love with you."

She laughed, loving the words even if they were beautiful nonsense.

"It's true," he countered, playfully pinching her chin. "Though I didn't know it then. I thought I'd been knocked senseless or something."

His mouth claimed hers, swallowing another rippling laugh.

She shoved her fingers into his hair, mussing tendrils free of the leather tie that held it back, not caring that whistles and gasps and throaty laughter erupted around them. They were *married.* They would make love tonight, and she could barely wait and she didn't care who knew.

Her heart lifted like a song.

"Enough of that—for now," Marie announced, tugging on Cecile's arm. "We're all starving. It's time to feast!"

With a cheer, the crowd gathered around the trestle table. Marie led Cecile to the head, while Sister Martha pulled Theo away to the foot. Cecile dug in her heels to follow him, but Marie held her fast.

"You are *not* sitting together." Marie raised her brows like Cecile had seen her do while scolding her toddler son. "If you do, you'll kiss and kiss, and you won't eat a bite. You'll need strength for the evening to come, Ceci, and it's my job to see you're properly fed."

This is what it is to be loved.

Overflowing with feeling, Cecile squeezed her friend's hand and slipped into a hard-back chair draped in a garland of red, gold, and russet leaves. Everyone else kicked a leg over the benches on either side of the trestle table. Wine had already been poured in tankards.

Etienne set the porcupine in the protection of the nearby woods and then jogged toward an empty seat on her left. Rather than sitting as the rest of the crowd already had, he seized his tankard and raised it.

"A toast," Etienne said, in a too-manly voice. "For my mother on her wedding day. And for the man she has chosen to marry." He swung his tankard toward the other end of the table. "The man for whom, from this day forward, I will call Father."

Delighted gasps rose up amid the crowd as Cecile struggled not to drown in an ocean of happy tears. She blinked and blinked, but Etienne's flushed and flexing features went blurry in her sight.

She reached for his hand. "I'm so—" *Hiccup* "I'm so proud of you, Etienne."

Etienne's tankard hit the table. He swooped down for a hug, burying his face in her hair. She wrapped her arms around him—they didn't quite reach anymore. She told herself it was the awkward angle, because she was seated and he bent over her. But she knew better. A thousand memories flooded through her.

Etienne as a boy sitting on her lap, smelling of mud and grass.

Etienne chasing grasshoppers in a field of hay, the sunlight shining on his head.

Etienne's high-pitched voice when he called her Mom for the first time.

Though her heart squeezed at thoughts of the boy now gone, she felt doors opening inside her, a wave of acceptance for something that had always been inevitable. Her sweet child had grown into a strong and honest man.

"Son."

Theo's voice, from just above them.

Etienne peeled away from her and loomed up, his fathomless black eyes uncertain as he looked at Theo.

Theo opened his arms.

A spasm crumpled Etienne's features, right before her son stepped into the embrace. Gasps and sniffs and sobs echoed up and down the table, followed by applause.

"Blessings to all of you," Marie said from mid-table as the intensity of the moment shimmered. "Sister Martha, if you could lead the prayer?"

Theo headed back to the other end of the table, clearing his throat more than once before sitting.

Etienne swung a leg over the bench, swiping his eyes as a grin lit his face anew.

How bright fate shone down upon them all—Cecile could hardly believe her good fortune.

After the blessing, Marie cried out, "Let's eat!" and Cecile startled as the person to her right slipped a slice of venison onto her plate.

"Red meat for you," Genny said, winking. "There's more of that coming."

Cecile slid a hand over Genny's deerskin sleeve and squeezed. They'd managed to talk a little at the tavern, but Cecile had wasted too much time scolding Genny for taking such a great risk by going into the fort courtroom.

Genny had just shrugged and joined in the tavern singing.

In the long separation, Cecile had almost forgotten how lively Genny was, so full of humor and confidence and life.

"No more dodging questions." Cecile released her friend and picked up a knife to dig into the meat. "How did you get involved in all of this?"

Genny shrugged, took a bite of a pumpkin fritter, and spoke around it. "André and I arrived a few days ago to pick up trading supplies." Genny dropped her knife and accepted the bread basket as it came around, taking a piece for herself and tossing a second slice on Cecile's plate. "Our plan had been to get our business done in Montreal quietly—and we'd done that. But since the captain's place is remote enough to be safe, I insisted on visiting Marie before heading west."

"Ah." Cecile glanced down the table to where Marie and Lucas bent their heads toward each other. "Marie arranged everything, didn't she?"

"She helped, yes, but she didn't lead the charge." Genny's eyes danced as she tilted her head toward the other end of the table. "Your Theo planned everything, and Etienne spread the word as far as Quebec. If the gathering of supporters hadn't set you free at the courtroom, Theo would have abducted you from the fort. With our help."

Genny gestured to André beside her. The two of them looked every lean inch like lifelong woods runners, fearless and up for any caper.

"To be honest," Genny said, "I was hoping we'd get to break you out. Then we would have led you and Theo into the wild to live with us in Chequamegon Bay. I miss you, Cecile."

"I miss you, too." As much as she'd live anywhere with Theo, Cecile was glad the plan had gone differently. Unlike Genny, she didn't think she would make a very good deep-wilderness wife. "The captain has offered us some land next to his. I think I'm better suited here."

"And I'm thrilled you've found a place to call home. That's what is most important, right?" With a wink, Genny deposited fried pumpkin fritters beside the bread and meat on Cecile's plate. "Eat up, now. That's a big man you've fallen in love with."

"My goodness." Cecile slid a glance Etienne's way, but her son only ducked his head to hide his grin. "You and Marie, you're both shameless."

Genny tilted back her face, bronzed and freckled, and laughed with her mouth open. How stunning her friend was. And how happy, too, she realized, as Genny glanced back to check on her babe, snugly strapped on a cradleboard propped up against a tree.

All three King's Girls, Cecile thought, were a thousand times blessed.

Feeling like a big floating fluffy cloud of joy, Cecile dug into the feast before her, chatting with Genny and André, noticing out of the corner of her eye how Etienne's gaze kept shifting down the table toward a raven-haired girl about his age.

Inevitably, her own attention was drawn to Theo at the far end of the table, where it stayed.

As the meal went on, sunlight poured bright streaks across the grassy field in front of Marie's stone cabin. The air took on a chill, the talk became softer, the sunlight more mellow, and the looks Theo cast down the long table brimmed with the kind of hungry expectation she'd thought she would see directed only at more fortunate women—and never experience herself.

More guests, welcomed by Marie, came out of the woods. Out of their rough-woven bags emerged musical instruments, some homemade, others gleaming with lacquer that could only have been brought from overseas. Soon, they filled the clearing with music, melodies of another world, another time, a beautiful idyllic place. She listened, her heart buoyed by the harmony within and without.

"Ceci."

She turned to find Theo half bowed beside her, holding out his hand, whispering, "Dance with me."

They whirled in circles toward an open space by the musicians. They spun about in rhythm to the ancient melodies, the dappled light fluttering over them.

The future vibrated between them, blasting away all the horrors of the past, melting away the last of the old terrors.

They might have danced for a moment, or an hour, she didn't keep track. At one point, the musicians paused, and, with a man whispering *one, two, three,* they played a new song, with wild vigor, a reel that gathered the whole company, whooping and clapping and spinning.

The first stars winked over the trees when Cecile finally stopped to catch her breath. Theo drew her away, teasing intent bright in his eyes. They'd made it halfway to the barn when Marie stepped in front of them.

"Not yet." She seized Cecile's arm and pulled her away. "You go on ahead to the barn, Theo. Cecile needs a moment with her friends."

Theo released her with exaggerated reluctance—and also a gleam of humor.

After all, they had forever.

"I promise," Marie whispered as she dragged Cecile toward the main cabin, "I won't detain you for long—and you'll thank me, after."

Inside the cabin, Marie led her to the bedroom where Genny, sprawled cross-legged on Marie's bed, jumped to her feet. Marie shut the door.

Cecile realized all at once that the three of them were alone together for the very first time *ever*.

Cecile looked at each of them, eyes narrowing. "What mischief is this?"

"No mischief." Marie grinned. "It's our job to make you presentable for your wedding night."

"Oh." Cecile drew in her shoulders as a wave of *wanting* rushed over her, tingling everything between her scalp and toes. "I thought all I had to do was take off my clothes."

Marie laughed. "Genny will help you with that."

"I can't do that." Genny waved up and down the satin brocade dress Cecile wore. "It's been ages since

I've dressed in anything but deerskin. I'll be useless with all those hooks and eyes and ties and grommets and ribbons—"

"Brush her hair out, then." Marie seized a horsehair brush from the bedside table and held it out to the redhead. "I'll get these clothes off her."

"Honestly." Cecile raised her arms, giving in to her friends with a smile. "I'm quite sure Theo knows how to undress me."

"He'll tear this pretty dress." Genny came up behind her and tugged out the pins in the roll Marie had so carefully set. "Marie and I have seen how that man looks at you. That satin wouldn't make it out of the barn intact."

Cecile's imagination bounded ahead of her. She had to bite her lower lip not to make a squealing noise.

"Better to wear that instead." Marie jerked her head toward the bed where a cloudy swath of translucent fabric pooled on the furs "Theo is welcome to tear that to his heart's content."

The women laughed, and Cecile couldn't help but laugh along with them.

"I apologize for not arranging better wedding-night accommodations," Marie said while making quick work of Cecile's bodice laces. "The barn is the best I could do on such short—"

"The barn," Cecile said, unable to hold back a smile, "is perfect."

"I thought it might be, you naughty girl. I've decorated it a bit, though it wasn't easy to make it look romantic."

"Marie, look," Genny said, poking her head around to pinch Cecile's cheek. "She's blushing."

Marie grinned. "Excellent."

"I don't think I've ever blushed in front of André." Genny returned to tugging the brush through Cecile's unbound hair. "If I was pink-cheeked, it was always because we'd just had a good romp."

Cecile blurted, "Genny!"

"Come now, you're not an innocent." Marie tossed Cecile's bodice toward a chair, leaving her in her shift and skirts. "None of us is a young girl anymore. My first night as a wife was certainly *not* my first night with Lucas. Oh, how I remember that first night—"

"For me, it was daytime." Genny waggled her brows. "In the middle of the woods."

Hilarity gripped Cecile. Her friends laughed along, and for one, shimmering moment, Cecile felt like a girl again, back at the Salpêtrière Orphanage, bouncing on a hay mattress, bare-legged and giddy, sharing secrets with Marie in the dim light of their dormitory, conspiring mischief in whispers with Genny.

To think the three of them hadn't known how strange—and how beautiful—their futures would be.

Cecile grasped Marie's forearm for balance as she stepped out of the skirts. "I'm so grateful for everything you both did today. I don't know how to thank you."

"You've already thanked me." Marie's eyes danced. "For agreeing to take up Lucas's offer and stay for the winter."

"That's your gift to *me,*" Cecile said. "How could we say no?"

"Good." Marie's gaze flashed toward Genny. "Genny is staying, too, at least until spring."

"What?" Cecile gaped at the redhead. "But shouldn't you and André go back west?"

"Once the ice closes in, we'll be safe here. Plus, there's a complication." Genny wrinkled her nose. "I've been having a powerful yearning for gooseberry jam, and, well…" Genny slid her hand over her belly "I've already eaten through two jars of Marie's best. This baby will be born in early spring."

Squeals, and jumping, and then Marie scolding Genny for jumping, and then Genny laughing with her mouth open and swinging Marie around. They paused only to yank off Cecile's old shift and wrestle the gossamer one over her head, giggling all the while.

Cecile wondered how she'd come to deserve all this happiness.

"A winter together." Cecile clasped both women's hands. "All three of us. That's the best wedding gift ever."

Footsteps came from the parlor, and after a light knock, the door swung open. Marietta poked her head around the edge, eyes widening at Cecile. "Oh, my. You look breathtaking."

"I look naked," Cecile corrected, glancing down to see that the firelight shone through the fabric.

Marie snorted. "Theo will be thanking us for that."

"He's waiting for you." Etta slipped in to close the door behind her. "Impatiently, according to my husband."

Cecile tugged at the delicate fabric. "I can't walk outside like this."

"Borrow my cloak." Etta pulled the tie at her throat, gathered the blue wool, and handed it to her. "If you leave right now, while everyone is dancing a reel, no one will notice you crossing to the barn."

Cecile swung the cloak around her shoulders and pulled the warm edges close. Marie tugged the hood over her head. Genny brushed some lint off the fabric. Their eyes had gone suspiciously wet.

"I think"—Cecile's face hurt from smiling—"I'm ready now."

Etta pulled the bedroom door open. Blowing kisses to her friends, Cecile swept through and pulled open the outside door to a blast of cool air and music. She ran across the porch in the darkness. Golden light winked through the cracks in the caulking of the barn.

She used that light as a compass as she raced, hurling herself toward Theo, and a bright and loving future.

THE END

Don't miss the other novels in the King's Girls Series

HEAVEN IN HIS ARMS: Book One

Struggling to survive on the streets of Paris, Genny agrees to a dangerous masquerade: She switches places with a King's Girl, a young noblewoman about to be shipped to the colonies. It's a risky venture with a high price—once overseas, Genny must marry a stranger....

THE WINTER HUSBAND: Book Two

Jailed for crimes unbecoming a lady, Marie yearns for liberty even as she refuses the one choice that will set her free: An arranged marriage with a frontier stranger. Then a brawny ex-soldier offers a more dangerous proposal. Spend one winter as his wife in name only, and come spring he will set her free…

A HUSBAND BY CHRISTMAS: A Novella

Orphaned and destitute, Marietta agrees to become a King's Girl, one of many women shipped to Quebec to be married to ungovernable settlers. Determined not to be rushed into matrimony, she challenges every bachelor to solve a riddle before courting her. The scheme buys her time—until the knotty riddle is solved by a most unlikely suitor....

ABOUT THE AUTHOR

Lisa Ann Verge is a critically acclaimed RITA© nominated author whose many novels have been published worldwide and translated into eighteen languages.

She started her career writing emotionally intense romance about sexy men and dangerous women, and now as **Lisa Verge Higgins** she also writes life-affirming women's fiction.

A finalist for RT Book awards five times over, Lisa has won the Golden Leaf and the Bean Pot, and twice she has cracked Barnes & Noble's General Fiction Forum's top twenty books of the year.

When not writing, she can be found hunting wild mushrooms, learning Turkish just for fun, and keeping track of her three adult daughters, whose adventures make life interesting.